Francis Charles Philips

A lucky young woman

Vol II: A novel

Francis Charles Philips

A lucky young woman
Vol II: A novel

ISBN/EAN: 9783743420076

Manufactured in Europe, USA, Canada, Australia, Japa

Cover: Foto ©Andreas Hilbeck / pixelio.de

Manufactured and distributed by brebook publishing software (www.brebook.com)

Francis Charles Philips

A lucky young woman

A LUCKY YOUNG WOMAN.

A Novel.

BY

F. C. PHILIPS,

AUTHOR OF "AS IN A LOOKING-GLASS."

IN THREE VOLUMES.
VOL. II.

London:
WARD AND DOWNEY,
12, YORK STREET, COVENT GARDEN.
1886.

A LUCKY YOUNG WOMAN.

CHAPTER I.

CLEARLY there was now nothing to be done but to leave St. Austell Towers with sufficient dignity to cover a retreat. Sir Hugo needed a couple of days to recover his self-possession, and of course he took them.

When an elderly gentleman has sustained an unexpected and severe reverse, when everything he has intended and done for the best turns out a failure, and when everybody else in the world is shamefully ungrateful to him, it takes him a little time to readjust his feathers, and to recover the genuine knack of his jaunty strut. Even the best and most scientific of prize-fighters is a little disconcerted when he finds himself being picked up by his second, from a good fair knock-down blow, and carefully assisted back to his bottle-holder. It is the duty, or used to be the duty, of that judicious functionary, to sponge his champion's face, to arrange his hair, or what there might be of it, to pat him on the back, to administer a stimulant, to apply soothing unguents to any particularly ugly wound, and so when time was called to " bring his man up smiling."

The luckless Sir Hugo sadly needed at

this juncture a bottle-holder to bring him up smiling. It was idle, of course, to go back and pour out his sorrows to Lady St. Austell. The campaign had ended in disaster, and the only thing remaining was to make the best retreat of which the circumstances admitted.

This Sir Hugo did. I do not think that the St. Austells were particularly sorry to be rid of him, or that he himself felt at all anxious to prolong his stay. The only two persons at all concerned in the matter were Marcia and Lady Austell, who had learned to like one another, and were to that extent sorry to part.

The leave-taking was consequently rather a flat affair, and I am bound to add that in the servants' hall there was a freely-expressed opinion to the effect that Sir

Hugo was no gentleman. Servants in big households are apt to take a mercenary view of guests, unless the smallness or the total absence of the usual tip has been compensated by courtesy. Sir Hugo on principle was never courteous to those whom he considered his inferiors. He held that it made them unduly independent. Neither in his pecuniary dealings with them could he be accused of too profuse a generosity.

"He is a horrible old bore!" said Lord St. Austell frankly, as the carriage drove off to the station. "But he is very tough, and has not seen the last of his innings yet."

"I think life has a little soured him," said her ladyship apologetically. "He ought to have done much better, but he has somehow fallen through."

"He is at the bottom anyhow," brutally rejoined the other, "and he can't well get much further. They tell me he is on his last legs. But he seems pretty comfortable in the sawdust, and I don't think things trouble him much. I wonder if his wife was at all like that daughter of his. If so, he must have had his old wig pulled once or twice in his life. Miss Conyers is a devilish fine girl, and it's a shame to see her life wasted in this kind of way."

"We all have our troubles," said Lady St. Austell, "and I daresay Sir Hugo has his own, like everybody else. He certainly is not as well off as he used to be, and he has now hardly anything left in life but his daughter."

"Then," replied his lordship, unsympa-

thetically, "he takes precious little care
of the little he has left, and isn't commonly
thankful to Providence for it.　You don't
come into the smoking-room, Emily, and
so you don't know.　But if there is one
thing upon which all the men in this
house are agreed, it is that Miss Conyers is
the nicest girl they have seen for years—
handsome, simple, straightforward, and just
the girl to make a good man a good wife.
And if there is any other thing upon
which they are agreed—and we haul one
another over pretty freely, I can tell you—
it is that Conyers himself is a selfish old
humbug, who would touch his hat to you
for a sovereign if he thought nobody else
saw him do it."

And there was a ring in this last
sentence which gave her ladyship very

distinctly to understand that the discussion might be considered as closed.

There was another conversation of a more general kind that day over the five o'clock tea. The young unmarried ladies were all extremely glad that Marcia should have gone. They had seen through her all along. The way in which she had tried to entangle poor Lord Norwich was in-famous. She was getting old, no doubt, and would soon be *passée*. It had been a last desperate attempt, but at the same time it was a very poor return for all dear Lady St. Austell's kindness.

And one young lady of strong and ad-vanced views, who had once or twice actually made a political speech from a platform, went so far as to say, with a clumsy attempt at being funny, that if there were many such young women about as Miss Conyers, we should need something like a close time for the protection of young heirs to entailed estates and large rent-rolls—an observation which, so to say, brought down the house.

It is within my knowledge that this lady herself next year led a victim to the altar in the form of the examining chaplain to the bishop of her diocese, after several desperate attempts to capture in their proper order of succession, the archdeacon, the rural dean, and the precentor.

We have all heard the phrase, "a good old garrison hack." But for downright spitefulness, without even the thinnest pretence of good-nature to cloak it, commend me to the elderly spinster, the Diana among the unmarried choir, in an old-fashioned cathedral town.

*　　*　　*　　*　　*　　*

It was a dull dreary journey from Oakshire to Euston. Sir Hugo made no pretence about matters. He was too furious with his daughter to be commonly civil to her, and too much afraid of her to bully her as he could have wished. He disliked reading at all times, and was far too careful of his eyes to read in a train. So he commenced by pretending to go to sleep, and was very soon asleep in real earnest.

Marcia, for her part, had quite enough to do at first in looking out of the windows. I think there is no greater sign of a healthy mind than to be able to take pleasure in scenery—I do not mean glaciers, and water-

falls, and other such triumphs of nature,
but plain, simple, ordinary English scenery,
such as Gainsborough loved to paint, and
which out of England can be found to its
greatest perfection in those portions of
southern France which are not yet fashion-
able or overrun with tourists.

So Marcia looked out of the windows
till it became dark. And then—for she
was not the kind of young lady to carry
knitting with her, or to bother herself
with a book-stall novel—she settled herself down in her corner, and began to
think.

It was not a pleasant retrospect over
which she had to travel. She had lost
what she firmly believed to be her only
chance of happiness in life, and had lost
it in such a manner as to put it beyond

the possibility of recovery. She could see nothing before her now except years of unhappiness with her father. The only escape from this was marriage, and marriage now was out of the question. You might, indeed, as well have suggested to her that she should enter an English convent; to take one extreme or to take another, that she should sing three songs a night at an East-end music-hall, each with its proper allowance of *double entendre* and gesticulation.

In a general kind of way she concluded that she must live on in Sloane Street, see as little of her father as possible; above all, avoid recriminations with him, and perhaps occupy herself with her brush or her pen, and so make sure of a little income of her own.

It was a barren prospect enough—joyless, hopeless, and in all human probability endless. She could not even feel of life as did the philosopher who remarked, *c'est peu de chose, mais—après—c'est tous ce que nous avons.* She was about as thoroughly unhappy as she ought to have been if she had deliberately and wilfully brought all her troubles upon herself.

Vague ideas occurred to her of taking up by way of anodyne some sort of regular work, with her father's permission or without it. She could teach, for instance, in the Sunday School of the parish church, or become a district visitor, or insist on drawing every day from the Elgin marbles. She might even set to work in earnest upon music. But all these ideas rather floated before her mind than definitely presented themselves in any practical shape. And ultimately, she too, in the most methodical manner possible, fell asleep.

She is not the only one among us who, without having read their Odyssey, or even their Tennyson, have longed without knowing it for the land of the Lotos-eater. The nearest approach to that land is sleep. I absolutely and flatly refuse to credit the story that Homer, undoubtedly a Levantine Greek, was also an opium-eater. Let any one who has ever known the effects of opium, ask himself in what they resemble the simple happiness of the followers of the King of Ithaca—when they first made trial of the magic flower.

London it was at last, with a dull, heavy November fog, out of which if you had hewn a sample with a knife, and cut a crayon from it, you would certainly have made a distinct stroke of malodorous grease upon a sheet of clean paper. There was a cab of the genus Noah's Ark to be procured for her father and for herself, and all the luggage had to be stowed upon the top of it, and then there was a dreary, dreadful drive down Tottenham Court Road, and along Oxford Street, to the Sloane Street vault; for the house looked through the fog like a mausoleum constructed from the designs of an economical architect, and the stone hall was cold and damp, and there was a sepulchral suspicion in the air, of mildew and other such unwholesome and unpleasant things.

The only relief was to be welcomed in this catacomb of a house by dear, honest, lovable Fräulein Dietz. Sir Hugo, who

had telegraphed from St. Austell Towers
for a fire in his room, retired at once,
without so much as a good-night, to
brandy-and-water and bed. He was too
empty of energy to make himself even
commonly disagreeable. This happily left
Marcia and the Fräulein to their own
devices. And the Fräulein took the weary
young girl up to her room, where also
there was a fire, and as women say, made
a fuss over her, to which Marcia for once
in a way did not object.

The cheery little woman made the deftest
and tenderest of ladiesmaids, and brushed
Marcia's heavy hair for her soothingly,
and trotted round about her, bent on
other little ministrations, and in fairy godmother fashion produced cheering tea and
toast with butter, and then as the fire

crackled and threw its light over the room, making even the dull ugly old furniture with all its dilapidations seem cheerful, the Fräulein talked volubly away, steadily refusing to enter upon anything serious until the morrow.

"We must have no tiresome talk to-night," said the little woman, with a determined shake of her little head. "No worries to-night. You shall tell me every-thing to-morrow over a good walk, or if the fog keeps on, say you are ill, and we'll spend the day up here together."

And the Fräulein clapped her hands, and then she kissed Marcia, and—to tell the homely truth—tucked her up, and looked to the fire, and the blinds, and the curtains, and the candle, and the matches, and so trotted away.

If ever there was a thoroughly honest soul in all Sloane Street, or for the matter of that anywhere else in this world, it was little Fräulein Dietz.

And when next morning London woke under a canopy of fog, in one quarter of which was a small, bilious patch, to just remind Londoners that there was such a thing as a sun in the universe, which in happier regions and under more favourable circumstances was occasionally visible to the eye, the Fräulein came again to her child, and again tended her, and when the house was quit of Sir Hugo for the day, came and sat with her in her room, and listened patiently to the whole story, the outlines of which she had pretty shrewdly guessed for herself before Marcia fitted them in.

VOL. II. c

"It will be all right yet, my dear," said the good soul. "I wish I could help things on a bit myself, instead of merely being able to see them. There is a capital word in your English, Marcia. We have very good words in German, but we should want something like twenty-seven syllables to bring home to our Teutonic minds the exact force and meaning of what I believe is called gumption. Now my gumption, Marcia dear, is like the familiar spirit of that funny old pagan, Socrates, which always managed to let him know when things were going right and when they were going wrong. And this same gumption of mine tells me that things are going right at this minute, and will end as well as can be."

Then the Fräulein paused, and twisted her forehead and the corners of her mouth into most uncompromising wrinkles, and shook her head viciously.

"Never mind about your father, my child. He is a short-sighted old gentleman, and buzzes about like a big fly in the window. The buzz sounds very terrible, but there is no sting. Wait. Everything comes to those who wait. Sleep in the wood and the Prince will come, as he does in the fairy tale, and wake you with the prettiest of kisses. Your Mr. Douglas is a gentleman with a stout heart, my dear—so at least I think. And if he is not, we will not break our own, or do anything else that is foolish. We will take care of one another. You shall look after the old woman, Marcia, and the old woman will put on her best spectacles and keep her eyes open and look after you.

What a merry little time we will have of it together. Do you remember Canning, who pokes fun at us Germans in his clever Anti-Jacobin — 'A sudden thought has struck me. Let us swear an eternal friendship' ? "

And at this even Marcia laughed, for high spirits are contagious. And with the laugh the eternal friendship was as completely ratified as if it had been a deed of indenture signed, sealed, and delivered, *secundum artem.*

The business faculty was strongly developed in Fräulein Dietz.

*   *   *   *   *   *

The next few weeks were perhaps the least eventful in Marcia's life, but certainly not the least important. Let me explain exactly what I mean.

When in the tropics you encounter a cyclone, the resources of your vessel and your crew are taxed to the utmost. You are in a hurricane that may last for an hour or more. You ride through it in safety. Then comes a deceitful period of calm, which does not hoodwink old navigators. A landsman would think that all was over, and would wonder at seeing every man at his post, and every brow beetled with anxiety. Foolish landsman! The cyclone has two motions. It is a great ring of hurricane of the most furious kind, rapidly rotating round its centre. But the whole ring has also a forward motion of its own, and is travelling at the rate of many miles a minute in a straight line. Suddenly, and with the least notice, its full frenzy will strike you on the other side. Surmount that danger and you are safe; omit to anticipate it, and you are lost.

After the return to Sloane Street, Sir Hugo, aware that an exhibition of temper at home would not avail him very much, or in any way retrieve the prospects which had once lain before his gaze, persistently sulked, with an almost feminine lack of dignity.

He lay in bed late, condemned with a vehemence unusual for him the quality of his tea and toast, grumbled even more over his hot water, and departed to his Club fully an hour and a half late. He was more or less permanently ill-conditioned.

Jack Tar, speaking of a man who is passing through a fever of this kind, will tell you that "he has got the hump"—a significant phrase, implying that he is sitting huddled together, with his shoulders arched up over his ears. If ever a man "had the hump" in this, and bore his burden with the minimum of resignation and the maximum of querulous, fussy ostentation, it was Sir Hugo.

As he showed himself in the morning, his features wore an air of resigned woe, as of a man misunderstood, rejected, reviled, and forsaken, a martyr without a crown, a saint with no prospect of a place in the calendar.

But his appetite remained sound, and enabled him to bear up against what must have inevitably overwhelmed a feebler constitution.

So much for Sir Hugo. Marcia meantime had nothing to do but to think, and to talk things over with the Fräulein. The thinking did not lead to much. She certainly had the world before her, but it was an ocean of which she had no chart. It might be her lot to "touch the happy isles," or it might be that the gulfs would wash her down. All she could feel was that she must trust in herself, and in herself alone. And the first difficulty was not insuperable.

Exactly as the son of a county gentleman, who is of the requisite height, strength, health, and youth, can always enlist, so Marcia knew that she could always obtain a situation as a governess if her father's future conduct rendered it impossible for her to remain at home.

She would, moreover, have several advantages. There would be a roof over her head, and a home of some sort, which she would enjoy of right and not as a favour. There would be regular work, which is the best of all anodynes for the heartache, and there would be the sense of independence. So far, then, the future was clear.

For the rest, her life was very much that, in its surroundings and atmosphere, if not in the incidents that had led up to its present crisis, of Mariana in the Moated Grange. There is very much of the Moated Grange about Sloane Street; there are the broken flower-pots crusted with thickest moss, the rusted nails hanging by shreds from the walls, and here and there the trees wearily throwing their shadow, if there be sun for a shadow, as if they had sinned in the tropics, and had been transplanted by way of punishment to this land of fog and frost and filth and mist—a land where all things seem hopelessly the same.

It is Tennyson who (in *In Memoriam*) calls Harley Street "the long unlovely street." But if Harley Street be longer than Sloane Street, which I doubt, I will maintain in disputation as a thesis against the ghost of Peter Cunningham himself, that Sloane Street, in spite of its few smart shops, is the more unlovely of the two. It is odd, I may remark, that, according to the same eminent antiquarian, Sackville Street, Piccadilly, is the longest street in London without a turning out of it. And the course of my story shall show that there is a certain philosophy in this remark. Certainly Sloane Street has many turnings, which take you to many and unexpected places.

"To live for ever in this horrible street," thought Marcia to herself, "would simply drive me mad." And yet she saw no possible means of escape. Andromeda chained to her rock was not more forlorn or helpless. And it made things worse that she had the common sense to realize matters, in a matter-of-fact kind of way.

Sir Hugo, with nothing on earth to ruffle the even tenor of his self-contained existence, might well live on for many years to come. Besides, Marcia, although devoid of any particular shade of superstition, was sufficiently a woman to hold, that for a child to speculate on the death of its parent is parricide in thought, and no less a crime than parricide in fact.

At times her thoughts would wander back to Douglas, and she would wonder vaguely whether they would ever meet again. For it would be idle to pretend that her wings had not been singed, although singed slightly. And at that moment Douglas would have been a most happy solution of all her difficulties. I am sure that if he had come to the house, in his own sudden, abrupt, peremptory, and forcible manner, and told her that he had changed his mind, and meant to marry her whether she liked it or not, she would have welcomed him.

But nothing of the sort happened. Mr. Douglas had no intention of changing his mind whatever. His recreations, such

as they were, never took him down Sloane
Street or into Hyde Park, so that, possibly
happily for both of them, however the
meeting might have turned out, they did
not cross each other's path.

But Marcia found out an odd little
amusement of her own. It was better than
district visiting, it was more interesting,
and it gave her material for distraction.
She wandered one day down Sloane Street,
through Sloane Square, and so strayed,
as sailors would have it, "west and by
south," until she found herself, without
knowing where she was, in the gardens of
Chelsea Hospital.

A portion of these are reserved as
allotments for the retired veterans, each
of whom has his little patch, rather larger
than billiard-tables, and cultivates it ac-

cording to his own fancy. Some of them are masters of rock-work, and as skilful in the art of fortification in miniature model as "my uncle Toby" himself. Others, of a botanical or possibly culinary turn of mind, devote themselves to asparagus, early peas, and other dainties. Others are sufficiently human to grow such flowers as will tolerate the London atmosphere— marigolds, dahlias, sweet peas, and other hardy annuals.

Marcia took to wandering among these allotments and cultivating the old men. They were picturesque to the eye, and in themselves a quaint study of human nature. She used to buy them tobacco and snuff, for which they were properly grateful. And then she would wander out into the lime walk, and so sometimes perhaps stroll over into Battersea Park, the most beautiful by far of the London parks and the least known. Or else she would make her way briskly home, through the wilderness of Lower Sloane Street and Sloane Square, and so fall back again upon her books, her music, her pencil, or her own thoughts.

CHAPTER II.

A FEW weeks after the return of Marcia and her father, a thing happened at Boodles which for some days, indeed for nearly a week, set all the old gentlemen in all the bay windows in St. James' Street solemnly shaking their heads, and made not a few of them distinctly nervous—in fact, so nervous as to positively spoil their habitual enjoyment of the good things of this life.

Sir Hugo, at about half-past two in the afternoon, had just finished the lunch which he sometimes made do duty for a dinner, thereby saving table-money, and enabling himself later in the day to devote to whist a mind unclouded by the somewhat soporific process of digestion.

He had finished the last glass of his pint of claret, and was arguing with the head waiter about his bill, which was, he insisted, sixpence too much. The matter, small as it was, seemed to ruffle him extremely, so that a sort of hush came over the room and everybody listened.

" I will not be insulted," said Sir Hugo. " I will have none of your insolence. You shall suffer for this. I will write at once to the committee and lay the facts before them. This impertinence shall cost you—"

Here Sir Hugo unaccountably stopped. The muscles of his face twitched. A sort of spasm shook him all over. He tottered for a moment to and fro, and then fell forward helplessly and heavily upon his face.

They picked him up and put him in a chair, and tried to force some brandy in a teaspoon through his set teeth, and tore off his collar and neck-tie and rubbed his hands; but it was all or no use. The doctor from Arlington Street who had been sent for came quickly across, put his finger on the pulse, and looked serious. He motioned silence, and for a few seconds they all stood round and looked on, turning their glances from the doctor and his patient to one another, and then back again to the doctor. All that could be heard was the ticking of the coffee-room clock. Mr. Gainer, the proprietor, came hurrying on to the scene, looking almost as astonished as on that memorable occasion when he was blown across his own kitchen by the force cf a gas explosion.

The doctor laid Sir Hugo's hand down, resting it gently upon his leg.

"He is dead," said he. "The heart has ceased to beat."

And then they all looked on Sir Hugo, and saw in his face that he was dead. And they broke up and gathered together in little knots of four or five, and talked in whispers for a few seconds, and so went one after another almost noiselessly from the room. The doctor was right. The troubles of this world will vex Sir Hugo no longer, and there is a vacancy in the list of members of the club which for so many years had practically been his home.

Before an hour was over the paper boys were calling out in the street, " Special edition. Sudden death of a baronet at a West End Club! Terrible excitement!"

There was no biography of Sir Hugo ready that evening in any editorial pigeon-hole. He had not been a person of sufficient importance. But at the offices of the *Morning Post*, his favourite paper, a deputy assistant sub-editor got down Debrett from the shelves, and "did" Sir Hugo in fourteen lines. Three lines more being needed by the exigencies of "measurement," he added that the deceased baronet, who was well-known in London society, had been for several years a member of the club in which the sad occurrence took place, and where his loss would be deeply lamented by a large circle of friends and acquaintances. The title, it was added, expires with him, the only representative of the family now surviving being his daughter, Miss Marcia Conyers, by his late wife Lady Conyers, who predeceased him by some years.

What effect had the melancholy intelligence upon Marcia? Exactly as much as might have been expected. A sudden death is always a terrible thing. But for years past Marcia and her father had had no tie to bind them together, unless it were the fact that they shared the same roof.

By his death she did not even lose a companion. Nor can it be said, on the other hand, that by it she gained her liberty. For her liberty was now valueless to her. The sole change made in her position by Sir Hugo's death was that it left her more than ever free, when it was too late, to choose her own course of life and to work it out for herself.

Sir Hugo's only two mourners were the doctor whom he usually consulted when it had pleased him to consider himself ailing, and the old family solicitor. Nor am I in a position to state who was responsible for the tombstone which recorded the dates of his birth and death, adding, according to the accustomed formula, that he was deeply lamented by a large circle of relations and friends. The payment of the undertaker's bill, which was sent in with business-like promptitude, left Marcia, according to Sir Hugo's solicitor, mistress of an exceedingly small balance at the bank, and a house full of dismal and faded furniture.

The man of law was kind enough to

arrange for the sale of everything that could be sold except her own books and trifles, and when Marcia was able at last to ascertain her exact position, she found that she was worth about four hundred pounds. Sir Hugo, it seems, had characteristically converted everything on earth to which he was entitled into an annuity. He would have included the furniture as well had it been possible to do so with the least advantage to himself, or the addition of even a five-pound-note to his annual income.

And thus Sir Hugo passes away from our history, having done as much mischief as was possible, without even the excuse of doing it from the best of motives.

* * * * * *

Almost immediately after the funeral,

and before the inevitable sale by auction, with all its unpleasant incidents, Marcia and the Fräulein went away together to a small seaside place where lodgings and living are cheap even in what is called the height of the season; and here for a week or two the Fräulein knitted elaborate works of art in Berlin wool, while Marcia boldly set to work to colour photographs, finding her own colours of course, for an eminent local photographer, who paid her sixpence a piece for the photographs, and a guinea for enlarged copies, or, as they are called in the trade, miniatures from the photographs.

These he retailed, the photographs half-a-guinea each, and the enlarged pictures, according to the credulity of his customers, from five guineas upwards.

Mean time the two ladies borrowed the

Times every morning from the circulating library and newspaper shop, and diligently answered every advertisement which announced that a governess was needed in a gentleman's family. And at the end of a week or so a definite result was obtained.

Mr. Huggins of the Stock Exchange and of Queen's Gate wanted a governess for his four daughters. The qualifications required were such as Marcia possessed. The fact that she was an adept in free-hand drawing and otherwise clever with her pencil and brush helped her considerably, Mr. Huggins being, like many other city men, a judge of pictures and a judicious purchaser, and anxious consequently that any little leaning towards art his children might have should be increased and developed.

And thus it came about that Marcia found herself installed at Queen's Gate, with a salary of actually seventy pounds a year, and with comforts about her such as those which she had seen for the first time in her life at St. Austell Towers. And there was another ray of pleasant sunshine in her life: for Fräulein Dietz had taken lodgings, two tiny little rooms, in one of those quaint nooks which still exist in Old Chelsea, and every now and then, when the children were taken by their mother in a body to a flower-show, or for a round of visits, or to some entertainment or other at the Hall which commemorates the many virtues public and domestic of the late Prince Consort, Marcia was free to run round to the Fräulein, and have one of those long talks about nothing and everything which seem somehow to soothe the female mind, exactly as it soothes a man to sit down opposite another man and to smoke a pipe with him in that solemn silence which is perhaps the very surest indication of mutual regard.

So that Marcia's life was now busy, useful, and independent, and consequently contented in proportion. "Live on a shilling a day and earn it," said Abernethy to the old nobleman who wanted that eminent physician to cure him of chronic indigestion. And with plenty to do, and the resolution to do it conscientiously and thoroughly, Marcia found her life far happier and brighter than she had ever hoped or expected.

Mr. Huggins had commenced life as a clerk. He was industrious and punctual.

For year after year he never asked for a week's holiday, and the only amusements he permitted himself were harmless and simple. He liked to go to the pit of the theatre, especially if he could get a free pass. He was also partial to harmonic meetings at old-fashioned public-houses, and would occasionally go so far as to consent himself to oblige the company with a song or perhaps a recitation.

But in his own way, and according to his own lights, he was ambitious. He had the sense to see that life is the pleasanter for many things which only money can give you. So it came to pass that one morning he very much astonished his employer, who paid him his salary weekly, by respectfully giving that gentleman three months' notice, intimating that he would be ready to leave his stool in the office sooner, or in fact at once, if his place could be filled up.

For Mr. Huggins had actually made about a thousand pounds, and had resolved to start as a jobber on his own account. While he was still a clerk, and with apparently no prospect of ever being anything more, he had married the present Mrs. Huggins, whose father kept a shop in Old Kensington, where he sold eggs, butter, dairy-fed pork, and other farm produce.

The two men made acquaintance at a select harmonic meeting held on the first floor of a large public-house, and the intimacy thus commenced progressed so favourably, that after he had dined a certain number of Sundays with the pork-butcher, Huggins, with that gentleman's consent, and in fact approbation, led his eldest daughter to the altar of Old Kensington Church.

The honeymoon was spent at Gravesend, and when the young couple returned, the pork-butcher did his duty as a man and a father, furnishing a house at Hammersmith, of which he purchased a seven years' lease, and otherwise substantially evincing his satisfaction.

It was not long after the marriage that Mr. Huggins, as we have said, was able to start in Capel Court on his own account. He had given his father-in-law some excellent advice, and had so secured that old gentleman's confidence. He knew the ins and the outs of the Stock Exchange to a shade. He was a cool-headed man, who never speculated except upon a certainty, or, as they say on the turf, never overlaid his book.

I have heard it said by a most eminent broker when discussing the mysteries of his craft, that early information combined with a large credit would ruin the devil in a month. Mr. Huggins stuck to solid business, and allowed others to pull the chestnuts out of the fire. And money is like a snowball. It is excessively difficult to make five hundred pounds. But it is not at all difficult, with patience, coolness, and a few other kindred virtues, to turn your five hundred pounds into five hundred thousand. And that is what Mr. Huggins did.

He had everything now that ought to have made him happy — everything, in short, that money can command. But as the greatest of all Roman poets has it, the *amari aliquid* was perceptible in his cup. He felt, as did the illustrious Mr. Boffin, that his wife's ways were not as his own. She had largely developed on the aristocratic side of her nature, while her unfortunate husband still retained his simple tastes; and when at the head of his own table, if he took the trouble to glance down the French *menu*, would think with a sigh of the days when he used to enjoy thoroughly his beef-steak and pickled walnuts with half a pint of port at the Jamaica coffee-house.

And when in the evening the distinguished professionals who honoured him with their company, and expected as a matter of course a twenty-pound-note to be sent to them the next morning, were pounding on the grand piano, or electrifying the company with the latest Italian *tour de force* for the lungs and throat, his mind used to wander back to the happy days when he used to hear the hammer descend upon the table, and the chairman's cheery voice call out, "Gentlemen, Mr. Jones will kindly oblige; gentlemen, give your orders. Silence, gentlemen, if you please, for the 'Death of Nelson.'"

Believe me, that in this life the truest pleasures are the simplest. What human being in the world is so happy for the moment as a child unexpectedly taken to see the horse-riders?

Mrs. Huggins, on the other hand, was now in all her glory. She had cut all her old friends and school acquaintances. She had no poor relations to trouble her. She was thoroughly content and satisfied

with herself.   It never occurred to her that
the society which frequented her *salons*
showed her consideration out of respect for
the sterling good qualities of her husband.
She fully believed herself a *grande dame*,
and made herself correspondingly ridiculous.

The daughters took after their mother,
and so far as nature had intended them for
anything, were admirably fitted to become
barmaids at a busy railway counter.

The eldest was nearly eighteen, and was
shortly to "come out."   Her name was
Catherine.   In the family circle she was
Kitty. In society, and at the foot of her
letters, she was Celia.   Prosperity had not
done much to improve her natural dis-
position or talents.   She was, in fact,
ingrainedly vulgar, and very superficially
veneered.   Her younger sisters were good-

natured, rough, and distinctly boyish in their tastes and habits. They had not yet been spoiled. Their names, for which their mother was responsible, were Victoria Maude, Honoria Alice, and Alexandra Louise. Victoria Maude would be sixteen her next birthday. The ages of the other two I cannot exactly undertake to give, but the elder was past fourteen, and the younger nearly twelve.

The life of a governess is, especially in a wealthy family, proverbially unpleasant. Marcia escaped many of its indignities. But it would be idle to pretend that she was happy; and to be merely comfortable is, for the young, at any rate, the smallest element in happiness.

A governess, after all, is rated on the ship's books by her wages, which are often

less than those of the cook, ladies'-maid,
and first housemaid. For a girl who is at all
proud, however rightly, or even sensitive,
the occupation is a slow torture, galling
to the last degree. And so Marcia soon
found it.

I could easily set out a list of the petty
things under which she had to chafe, with
nothing to console her except the knowledge that she was doing her work honestly
and thoroughly. But I forbear the recital,
as it would be unintelligible to any man
who may happen to read this history, and
for any woman wholly and absolutely
unnecessary.

When I was a child there used to be a
story in my History of England about
Alfred in the swineherd's hut, and I have
often wondered whether it ever, amid her

present surroundings, came up in Marcia's mind as it very well might have done. I have always gathered from the story, by the way, that the swineherd himself was a very decent kind of fellow, but desperately in terror of his wife.

One incident occurred to break the otherwise monotonous current of her life. John Douglas, hearing of Sir Hugo's death, or seeing it in the papers, called at Sloane Street, to find the carpets and hearthrugs hanging in the balconies, the walls placarded with posters, men running about in aprons and slippers, and all the other symptoms of a sale.

He saw the auctioneer's foreman, and gave that dignified person instructions to buy in for him several things which he felt certain Marcia would value. The most important among them was a large oil-painting, which spoke for itself as the portrait of her mother. The remainder were trifles which, with the instinct of a lawyer, he could detect as being valuable in Marcia's eyes, and in some cases possibly sacred.

Then, through the auctioneer, he found out the family solicitor, and through that gentleman easily ascertained where Marcia was staying. He then wrote her a letter of condolence—as simple and manly a letter as need be—and made arrangements to have his purchases put at her disposal. The letter was answered, and Mr. Douglas warmly thanked, and then the correspondence stopped ; and Marcia, having obtained from Mrs. Huggins a somewhat ungracious consent, was enabled to make her own room more of a home by arranging in it the treasures thus happily rescued.

Mr. Huggins himself was pleased to inspect the picture, and to pronounce his opinion that it was an admirable work of art, and so far as he could judge must have been a striking likeness of the lady herself. He was reprimanded for this by his wife, who told him roundly that the master of the house had no business to encourage a young woman in his service by chattering to her, and that for her part she thought a big picture like that was not at all the kind of thing for the bed-room of a governess who knew her position.

After this incident Marcia's life went on with terrible regularity and precision· What is the daily routine of a governess? The life of a city clerk from nine in

the morning until five or six is absolute
and unfettered liberty to it. He has, at
any rate, his two daily journeys, his half-
hour for lunch, the companionship of his
fellow-clerks, and his entire evening to
himself.

The governess has to rise early. She
must breakfast with her pupils, and put
them through dress parade. Then come
lessons, and a walk in the park, and early
dinner. Then, if it be fine, a walk again,
or if it be wet more lessons of a light
character. Then there is tea—and then her
evening is her own, unless the mistress of
the house can either find or invent something for her to do.

There is a point beyond which it is not
wise to irritate your cook. But out of your
governess you can, as the saying is, " take

it"; and ladies with any sense of what is due to themselves are apt to take it out of the governess very relentlessly. Her real rest is the half-hour before she falls asleep.

There is a peculiarity about sleep. If you are happy and contented with your position, you go to sleep the moment you have gone to bed. Soldiers and sailors can do this. Life sits lightly upon them.

Marcia slept now from very weariness, but it was not the wholesome sleep from which you wake refreshed. And often, as she lay thinking, she would hear the clocks chime hour after hour, until the sparrows, for whom she put stray crumbs upon her sill, would come to twitter over their meal, and through the London skies would struggle the London day.

CHAPTER III.

ONE morning occurred an incident which materially altered the whole course of Marcia's hitherto placid if dreary existence under the roof of the *famille* Huggins.

She was walking with the children in Hyde Park. They had made their way to Albert Gate, and were strolling among the little nooks of rockery and fern and waterwork, when they were overtaken by Lord Norwich, who had been breakfasting at Knightsbridge Barracks, and was strolling along with his host and a companion, both

in uniform. None of the three was in a
hurry. They were, in fact, leisurely discussing the prospects of certain horses who
had done well last autumn, and were now
prominent in the betting for the Two
Thousand and Derby.

Hastily excusing himself, Norwich left
his companions and went straight up to
Marcia, whom he had not seen since they
were at St. Austell's Towers. Then there
was about three minutes' conversation of the
recognized and conventional type. Lord
Norwich had, of course, been greatly shocked
and distressed to learn of Sir Hugo's death.
He was extremely happy to meet Miss
Conyers again. He would do himself the
honour of leaving his card in Sloane Street,
and so on. And then the conversation
became less formal and more natural.

Marcia had to tell Lord Norwich as briefly as she could all that had happened to her since they last met, and to explain her present position and occupation. Then came a discussion as to whether Lord Norwich could call upon her. Marcia, of course, saw that this was out of the question. An ex-guardsman, still a bachelor, cannot consistently with the recognized proprieties pay morning visits to a nursery governess. So ultimately it was arranged that Lord Norwich should find out somebody who knew the Huggins, and should, as he emphatically put it, " work the oracle " in that way.

" There are one or two fellows in my old regiment," said he, " who are the sons of city men, or somehow connected with the city. The thing ought to be easy enough.

Let me set about it in my own way, Miss Conyers, and we will soon see. And I can only say that it gives me real pleasure to know that we now are not likely to lose sight of one another. It will certainly not be my fault if we do."

And with this they shook hands, and as Lord Norwich walked away with his old brother-officers in one direction, Marcia and her charges pursued another.

This is exactly what happened; the whole of what happened, and nothing more. But Marcia's pupils took the story home to their mother, and without the least intention of doing mischief were singularly unfortunate in their account of what had taken place.

Mrs. Huggins learned to her horror that Marcia had been talking to soldiers in the

Park. There are plenty of persons who are firmly persuaded that the publicans mentioned in the New Testament were none other than licensed victuallers ; and when the pork-butcher's daughter was informed that her governess had actually been walking and talking with a companion of common soldiers, presumably a common soldier himself, if not indeed something much worse, she composed herself to that peculiarly feminine state of mind in which a lady feels herself counsel for the prosecution, principal witness for the prosecution, judge to sum up to the jury, jury to act upon the judge's advice and convict out of hand, and judge again to pass sentence in the most approved style.

Accordingly she summoned Marcia to her presence, and promptly opened fire upon her.

"I am shocked beyond measure, Miss Conyers," began the matron; "shocked and greatly disappointed—for I had a very favourable character with you—to find that you have actually while in charge of my children been talking to a lot of common soldiers in the Park. I never heard of anything so disgraceful! It is what one might expect from the nursemaid, if you sent her out with the perambulator, exactly what you might expect; but I certainly never expected anything of the kind from you."

"I think, madam, you are mistaken," answered Marcia.

"Don't 'ma'am' me, Miss Conyers," replied the lady, with a dignity that would have irresistibly set you thinking of Juno in a burlesque; "don't 'ma am' me. Perhaps you will next ask me to believe that my own dear children are story-tellers."

"I do not ask you to believe anything of the sort, Mrs. Huggins," said Marcia, losing her temper in her turn; "the children have no doubt told you exactly what happened; but the gentleman who spoke to me was Lord Norwich, whom I met a few months ago when I was staying at Lady St. Austell's with my father. Who Lord Norwich's friends were I do not know, but I saw from their uniform they were officers in the Guards."

Now this was a facer for Mrs. Huggins. She was altogether unequal to the occasion. Evidently she had made a mistake if Marcia was telling the truth. Clearly if Marcia were not telling the truth she was a very wicked and designing young woman.

Ladies of the stamp of Mrs. Huggins are apt to be illogical in their ill-temper. The best way out of the difficulty was to assume that Marcia was telling falsehoods, so Mrs. Huggins looked unutterable things, and with an intimation that she should lay the matter before Mr. Huggins that evening swept out of the room.

Now Mr. Huggins, although usually deferring to his wife for the sake of peace and quietness, was apt at times to speak his mind, and to speak it plainly.

"You must be a born fool, Maria," said the stockbroker in a tone his wife knew, and of which she was secretly afraid; "the girl's a lady as much as yourself. Why on earth should she tell you lies about the matter? Old Sir Hugo was a swell, and knew more lords than you or I know the names of.

I dare say the girl thinks no more of a lord
than you do of a lord mayor. You just
get that black monkey down off your
shoulder, and be civil to the girl. We
know a lord or two as it is, but we could
afford another. Go and make it up with
her, and let's have this young swell's legs
under my mahogany. The girls are coming
on, and I could manage to do the handsome
if one of them married well. Who knows
what may happen?"

And having delivered himself of this,
for him, unusually long allocution, Mr.
Huggins strode off in a bit of a temper
to a den which he called his library, where
he kept a few old books, a box or two of
cigars, and a cellarette.

Mrs. Huggins did not like the rebuke any
the better because she saw the justice of it.

It struck in her gizzard, to use her own words, that she should have to eat humble pie to a governess. But she knew her husband far too well to risk disobeying him when he was evidently in earnest.

So she made Marcia a lame and most ungracious apology, explaining that she was suffering that morning from one of her bad headaches, and she then plunged at once into diplomacy.

" Mr. Huggins and myself, Miss Conyers, have every wish that you should see your own friends, so far of course as is consistent with the proper discharge of your duties as governess, and Mr. Huggins wishes me to say that he is quite agreable that Lord Norwich should call here. In fact some friends of his were on the very point of introducing us. So that it will perhaps be as well if you write to his lordship and enclose an invitation to dinner."

Now here it was actually suggested to her to do the very thing which Lord Norwich had himself promised to arrange. It was difficult to know what to say. Marcia pointed out to Mrs. Huggins that she could hardly write to Lord Norwich herself, or invite him to a house which was not her own.

"Then I'll tell you what we'll do," said Mrs. Huggins, who was now quite keen in the matter, and most anxious to retrieve her blunder; "Mr. Huggins and I will send his lordship a dinner-card for the week after next, and I shall write upon it, to meet Miss Conyers, and you shall address the envelope. We'll make it the week after next, so as to make sure of his coming." And to this Machiavellian stroke of diplomacy Marcia could only give an unwilling consent, recollecting that after all Lord Norwich did not know her handwriting, and would so conclude that the card came from Mrs. Huggins herself.

And next day the Huggins family was in the height of its glory. For a groom with a cockade in his hat came round and left a polite note of acceptance; and it took Mr. and Mrs. Huggins some hours to settle the lists of their guests, and to fashion a suitable party to meet, as Mrs. Huggins proudly observed, a peer of the realm.

However the thing was done. The chief of the notables was a very worthy Manchester warehouseman, Sir Nathaniel Styles, who for his sins had been knighted during his year of mayoralty. Then there was the vicar of the parish, who had to be asked because his curate, the Honourable and Rev. Duodecimus Stapylton, was absolutely necessary, and could not well be asked, so the Huggins thought, without his chief. The family doctor, a sufficiently well-known practitioner at the West End, and the family solicitor, whose chambers were in Lincoln's Inn Fields and his suburban villa at Highgate, were added to the list. The rest were city men in a large and solvent way, one of them being Prime Warden for the year of the Ladle-makers' Company, while another, a distinguished soapboiler, was also a Governor of St. Bartholomew's Hospital. So that, as Mrs. Huggins reflected and in fact proudly observed to her spouse, the company was as good as any man in his senses need desire, and better than nineteen people out of twenty had any right to expect.

Into the story of all the anxieties which the arrangements of the banquet involved Thackeray would have delighted to enter. An eminent West End cook and confectioner sent round a trusty lieutenant with a couple of kitchen-maids, who had *carte blanche* given them for three days, and exercised the privilege as freely as it was given.

On flowers and fruit and other such things no expense was spared. Celia and Victoria Maude accompanied by their mother had a long and very satisfactory interview with that most distinguished milliner, Madame Hortense of Upper Brook Street. Mr. Huggins gave his mind to the wines and liqueurs, this being the one part of the business he thoroughly understood. The rare and choice fruits for the dessert

were left to the skill and judgment of
Mr. Nehemiah Isaacs of Covent Garden
and Bond Street, whose foreman also
undertook the appropriate decoration of
the table and of the room generally with
exotics.

Mrs. Huggins was in the seventh heaven
of gratified vanity. Never before had she
known her husband relax his purse-strings
so ungrudgingly. Mr. Huggins was also
pleased in his own quiet way to have the
chance of letting his city friends see that
he knew a lord—and no ordinary lord
either, but one with an old title, and,
as Mr. Huggins tersely put it, "pots of
money."

For poor lords are held cheap in the city,
where not a few of them condescend to add
to their limited incomes by guinea-pigging.

As for Miss Huggins and Miss Victoria Maude Huggins, they were dazzled with the splendour of the raiment they were to wear, and bewildered with dim visions of what might possibly happen if things were only to turn out as they do in fairy stories with a young prince and fairy godmother.

And so the hours went busily on till the fateful evening came.

I need not describe the meal. It was everything that could be desired. I am told that if you give the *chef* at the Travellers' discretion, and politely tell him that you leave the whole thing to his better judgment and experience, you can get the best dinner in London. Among city feeds that of the Goldsmiths' is undoubtedly the best, and next perhaps ranks that of the Fishmongers, while the Vintners are not far behind, and give a character to their banquet at the right season by serving up a swan.

Occasionally, too, a city man who is planning a good swindle, or has successfully carried a good swindle through, will invite his confederates to a private spread at the Ship and Turtle or the Albion. Mr. Huggins deliberately resolved not to emulate these noble repasts, but to eclipse them by a banquet such as that given by the happy owner of the "Golden Butterfly" at the Langham to the representatives of literature and art.

More than this I need hardly say. The dinner was one to be remembered. Delmonico himself would have expressed approval of it, and its cost per head made Mr. Huggins proud to think that he could do that kind of thing if he chose once a week without troubling himself.

Everything passed off as such dinners usually do. The men eat with discretion. The ladies eat recklessly and of everything, as is often the female habit. When the wine had made one circuit of the table and the fruit had been considered and admired, Lord Norwich, by virtue of his proximity, did duty at the door, and the ladies swept by him in gorgeous procession. Marcia, in mourning for her father, wore plain black silk, with a little collar of old point lace. Beyond this, although she had no ornament of any kind, as Talleyrand said of Lord Castlereigh, she was " *bien decorée.*"

Then came rare vintages and liqueurs, and choice cigars and coffee had to be sent in several times, for the men found the

wine good, and were disposed to linger over
it. When at last they filed up the great
staircase with that peculiarly sheepish look
which Englishmen have when joining the
ladies, Lord Norwich was doomed to dis-
appointment. Marcia had disappeared.

"You see, my lord," said Mrs. Huggins,
"Miss Conyers is still far from strong, and
she rises early. Else I should have asked
her to stop and play, for I am told she has
a very good touch."

His lordship, being unable to shrug his
shoulders, could only murmur some general
expression of regret. But, as I have before
had occasion to observe, he was a young
gentleman of rather more than ordinary
intelligence, and certainly able to make a
very shrewd guess as to how matters stood.
The opinion he expressed at the Guards'

Club some hours afterwards was vigorous. It did Mrs. Huggins justice, and I am sure that Mr. Huggins himself would have chuckled if he could have heard it.

However, Lord Norwich called in a day or two and left his card, and the little bits of pasteboard were reverently looked at and conspicuously deposited on the top of many other pasteboards in a large china bowl in the drawing-room. And Mrs. Huggins became gracious to Marcia: For a lord is a lord after all, and this one was a lord of the right sort, and it was consequently just as well to do a little to make Miss Conyers contented and willing to remain. Anyhow, nothing could be gained, as Mrs. Huggins tersely phrased it, by putting the young woman's back up. "Besides," the worthy matron incidentally remarked to her husband,

"Miss Conyers, I am quite sure, has a temper of her own, and it would be foolish at present to rough her up. We must see how things go, Mr. Huggins." And in the soundness of this policy Mr. Huggins was pleased to express his entire concurrence.

To wait and see how things would turn up was, from his point of view, the very perfection of all worldly wisdom. There is no knowing what may happen if you will only wait; or as they say in the city, if you can afford to hold on.

So it was decided between Mr. Huggins and his spouse that they should hold on. "There's no hurry, my dear," sagely observed the stock-jobber; "things may turn out as you and I should wish, or they may not. Anyhow this young swell is a good fellow, and a good card to play.

There's no reason why he shouldn't take a fancy to Celia, who is a monstrous fine-looking girl, very like what you were when you were her age. And though I say it who shouldn't, he might do a deuced deal worse. He wouldn't be the first lord anyhow who's married the daughter of a self-made man, and not done so badly by it either."

And Mr. Huggins rubbed his hands, and allowed himself for a moment to think how much he was worth. This was an enjoyment in which he seldom indulged, being, like many other rich men, superstitious, and holding that it brings bad luck to think of what you have already made, and distracts you from the plain path of duty, which is to think how you can make more.

CHAPTER IV.

LORD NORWICH did his duty like a man, and called upon the Huggins family more often than was absolutely necessary, so that Mrs. Huggins was intensely gratified, and in fact began to let not a few of her old friends fully understand the social distinction which had befallen her household ; whereat, with all the truly Christian spirit of the average British matron, the friends in question said spiteful things to one another about Mrs. Huggins behind her back, one of them indeed so

far forgetting what was due to her own
position in society as to refer to a vulgar
but not the less pungent proverb about
silk purses and the ears of female swine.
But these amenities did no harm, and even
if they had come to the knowledge of Mrs.
Huggins would probably have found her
too happy to be seriously ruffled by them.

But an incident occurred, small in itself,
and yet resembling one of those trifles
which are believed occasionally to make
and unmake empires and dynasties. It was
simply an outbreak of whooping-cough
among Marcia's pupils.

The family doctor at once ordered
change of air, and so off Marcia and the
children were packed to Eastbourne, together with a nurse, a ladies'-maid, a
landau and a pair of horses.

This Hegira distressed Mrs. Huggins
not a little, for Lord Norwich of course
had to be left in Town exposed, as Mrs.
Huggins sadly thought, to the machina-
tions of every designing mother and every
forward young lady whom he might meet.
Her only comfort was to reflect that he
had promised her tickets for the next
Guards' ball.   Beyond this she felt there
was nothing left but to put her trust in
Providence.

At Eastbourne, of course, there were
no lessons. This in childhood is, together
with fruit and other such luxuries, the
great consolation for illness. Thus Marcia
had very much of her time to herself, and
when the landau went out with the family
for the regulation drive, was entirely her
own mistress.

How she utilized these precious hours can easily be guessed. She set to work heart and soul upon a sea-piece. It gave her something to do, which was in itself a distinct gain. But as the work grew under her hands her soul entered into it, and she laboured at it with all her heart.

There is no amount of labour or enthusiasm too great to be given to a picture. Nor was there ever yet a really good picture that was dashed off. Marcia knew this and worked patiently.

Mrs. Huggins condescended to raise no objections. The governess, she thought, might as well be painting during such time as she had to herself as doing anything else. It was in fact more or less laudable in her to do so, as painting is a very proper accomplishment for a finishing governess, from whom it would not be the correct thing to expect plain needlework or anything useful.

As for the possibility that the picture might have any merit in it, such an idea never for a moment crossed Mrs. Huggins' mind. Mrs. Huggins had heard, of course, of Miss Thompson and of Rosa Bonheur, but would have been puzzled to tell which of the two it was painted soldiers and which cattle, and when she went to the Academy, which she regularly did, she looked solemnly at the pictures other people looked at, and so, like Tennyson's Northern Farmer, "came away."

And thus it came about that Marcia was actually able to get her picture finished during their stay at the seaside.

Now it so happened that Mr. Huggins

on one of his weekly visits had noticed
the picture in the school-room, and like
a wise man held his tongue about it until
he got a chance of talking to Marcia
alone. Then he gave her some really
kind and sensible advice.

"It's a good picture, Miss Conyers," he
said. "Take my advice; send it quietly
in to the Academy. It's a small one,
and very likely to be hung. Besides, you
have never exhibited yet, and nobody
can possibly be jealous of you. I know
those painters. They're as bad as actors,
and worse. They hate each other like
poison. You'll be skied, I'm afraid, but
send it in; and look here"—and here he
dropped his voice from habit, lest perad-
venture the wife of his bosom might be
within ear-shot—"here's my card"—and

he produced a card and pencilled a few words on the back of it. "When we get back to Town take this to Moss at Knightsbridge, close by Albert Gate. He'll varnish the picture for you, and put it in a proper frame. There's a deal of knack in choosing a suitable frame. And he'll send it in for you, and take all the trouble off your hands. And look here, Miss Conyers, I'll bet you twenty pounds to sixpence it's not rejected. Come now; take the bet for luck."

Marcia did not exactly see where or how the luck lay in the bet, but she felt sure that Mr. Huggins meant kindly; she thanked him warmly, and allowed him to produce his pocket-book and solemnly make an entry in it.

I will abbreviate a story which many

writers have told before me, each after his own fashion. Marcia finished her picture, and it was in due course sent, or rather taken round by herself, to Mr. Moss. That gentleman, who knew literally nothing about pictures except how to buy them and sell them (and a useful knowledge too), was pleased to express himself in terms of the highest admiration. He did his duty by the picture, for Mr. Huggins was one of his best patrons. It was properly strained, varnished, framed, and sent in, and then happened what might reasonably have have been expected, and exactly what Mr. Huggins had predicted.

The picture was a small one, and a good one. Marcia, being wholly unknown, had no enemies. It was accepted, and hung in one of the small rooms. So much was due to its merits.

It exactly filled up a small place near the line, and there the hanging committee put it. This was Marcia's luck.

It was really almost in the fitness of things that this poor child should have a stroke of luck at last. But there was better luck to come. Marcia, by Mr. Huggins' advice, put herself entirely in the hands of Mr. Moss. Mr. Moss, for some inscrutable reason of his own, put a reserve price on the picture of a hundred guineas. Good old Mr. Huggins was determined it should not go for less, and he chuckled to himself over his glass of grog.

" Money well laid out," he said ; " do the girl good, and do me no harm. Why should I let her take a ten-pound-note or three fivers for it? She'll have made her mark in four or five years, and the picture will be worth double the money if I buy it myself. I can easily hang it up in the city. Maria never comes there, and I like to encourage young talent "—a generous sentiment, which Mr. Huggins emphasized with a good warm-hearted imprecation.

And now to tell the story of the picture. Lord Norwich, who of course called at Queen's Gate as soon as the family returned from Eastbourne, heard of the picture, and went straight off to the Academy and made the arrangements for its purchase.

That evening Marcia over her tea in the schoolroom received a letter from Burlington House, to tell her that the picture had been sold at the reserve price to a gentleman who had made the purchase through an

agent; that it had been duly starred, and
that the money was at her disposal.

A hundred guineas! One hundred and
five pounds! Marcia had heard of such
news before, but to find this amount of
wealth at her immediate disposal actually
bewildered her.

Her first proceeding was to write to her
dear old Fräulein, and tell her of the good
news. Her next was to make an excuse for
going up to Burlington House. Then there
was of course the business of identification,
and when this was completed, and Marcia
had satisfactorily made out that the picture
was hers, and that she was herself, she had
only to leave the secretary's room with a
cheque. The secretary at her request made
it open with a few words of warning as to
the risk.

The cheque, which was on the Bank of England, was buttoned up in the palm of Marcia's glove, and the bank-notes into which it was converted were also securely taken back to Queen's Gate in the same manner. But the journey back was delightful, for there were one or two little purchases to be made, and Marcia was not above the weakness of a harmless love for shopping.

That evening a number of people were made happy in a small way. Marcia confined her gifts, of course, to her pupils, to the ladies'-maid, housemaid, and cook, together with the gentleman who attended to the door and waited at lunch, and a younger gentleman in buttons and a jacket. But the pleasure in the lower regions was universal, and the butler did honour to the occasion

by the production of a peculiarly choice
bottle of port, which was pleasantly discussed in the housekeeper's room.

Now it so happened (for the Fates rule
the affairs of men, and there are a few men
who meddle a good deal with the Fates,
giving those three worthy spinsters no
little trouble over the tapestry-frame) that
Lord Norwich some few days after his
eventful purchase found himself at
Tattersall's. Having concluded his business
at that rendezvous he decided to call at
Queen's Gate, and did so. He was shown
into the drawing-room, where Marcia was
making herself useful by sorting and
arranging some music.

Marcia was about to leave the room, but
Lord Norwich would not hear of it. He
said that he wanted to talk to her about

her picture, and he had just entered upon the subject when Mrs. Huggins rustled into the room. That lady was in a state of the greatest trepidation and bustle. For she had apparelled herself hurriedly, and was uneasy as to her general outfit and rigging. Start your yacht at a minute's notice. The next twenty minutes are a period of terrible anxiety. You cannot tell what may happen at any moment. A spar may snap or be " carried," or something else equally important may, in nautical phrase, give way.

At balls and archery-meetings and lawn-tennis tournaments, a piece of tape or even a button has been known to give way with unforeseen and disastrous consequences. And Mrs. Huggins felt uneasy as to the general condition of what yachtsmen would have termed her running-gear. This uneasiness was exasperated by the fact that Marcia and Lord Norwich were chatting together in a manner which the worthy matron afterwards described as brazenfaced.

Mollified for a moment by the manner in which his lordship paid his respects to her, Mrs. Huggins purpled with suppressed indignation at his first remark.

"I was congratulating Miss Conyers," he blurted out in his own schoolboy's way, "upon her success at the Academy. It is really one of the successes of the season. More by luck than judgment, as I acted on the advice of a friend who writes art criticism for the papers and paints a bit himself, I happen to possess the picture, and am very fond of it. I suppose, Mrs. Huggins, that you have seen it at the Academy yourself?"

At this frank and light-handed " lead off
with the left," Mrs. Huggins, in the classical
phraseology of sporting circles, " saw stars."
Her horizon was bewildered. A mine had
been sprung upon her. Her governess, her
paid governess—not the governess of anybody else, but her own white slave—had
been daring to have leisure, and in that
leisure to paint pictures. This was well
enough, if allowed upon sufferance. Your
governess may practise with her pencil.
This so far was well enough. Your
governess may practise with her pencil
exactly as she may practise on the piano.
It is her duty in that station of life to
which it has pleased Providence to call
her, that she should make herself a pro-
ficient by private practice in her own
menial arts, exactly as your groom acquires

a better seat if he trots about in the morning upon one of the carriage-horses with nothing under him but a rug, and leads another horse by the bridle. But he must do this always in a proper and dutiful spirit, and with no eye to his own prospects in life, recollecting that it would ill become him to set up on his own account as a livery and stable-keeper or a riding-master, when his own master and mistress have always been most kind and considerate to him.

But for a governess to paint on her own account—to steal the time of her employers, and to repay them by the basest treachery —what was the world coming to, thought Mrs. Huggins? And she quivered with indignation.

"I knew," she said, with just as much

stiffness as she dared assume towards a "live lord," "that Miss Conyers was considered clever at painting. But I was not aware that she did more in that way than to qualify her for her position in life. Mr. Huggins himself is a very good judge of pictures, and several Royal Academicians are among our most intimate friends. Miss Conyers can hardly hope to do more than employ her talents in teaching, and it would be a mistaken kindness on the part of her friends to raise her hopes."

This emphatic "gentlemen of the jury, consider your verdict," fairly staggered Lord Norwich. "What was I to say?" he afterwards asked. "I remarked that talent of any kind was a great gift, and that I wished I had any talent of any kind myself. And then said that an artist's life

must be a very jolly one, and that I myself
would sooner be an artist than a—yes! I
was actually going to say governess.
Luckily I pulled myself together just in
time, and stumbled out with guardsman,
which was about all I had ever been fit
for. And then I felt I was only getting
deeper into the mud. So I collared my
hat and took my hook."

These were the unhappy young man's
exact words, and they represent with
sufficient accuracy his exact condition of
mind.

When he was fairly out of range of Mrs.
Huggins, and the big street door had shut
behind him, and he found himself in the
street, his lordship whistled—a long, low
whistle, all upon a single note. As he had
no dog with him, the baker's boy whom he

passed stood still, and then turned round and stared after him.

"Another swell gone wrong," said the baker's boy. "They always *will* overlay their book." And the baker's boy went on.

Inside the great house in Queen's Gate Mrs. Huggins did not whistle. Whistling was not among her accomplishments. But she behaved as a wife and a mother and an ornament of society ought to have behaved under such shameful circumstances.

Her anger had hitherto been suppressed. Now it blossomed out, and her face assumed a hue of mottled crimson and white, something like that of Castille soap. She armed herself with her smelling-bottle, went straight to the library, took up her position on the hearthrug, with her back to the fire, and sent word that Miss Conyers was to come to her at once.

When a man intends to insult you, he stands himself and orders you to sit down. This is a relic of the days of the small sword. It means, "I am a gentleman, and shall not take you at a disadvantage. But, at the same time, my moments are precious; I should waste them if I had to sit down and get up again."

When a woman wishes to insult you, she sits down, and by command, or otherwise, intimates that you are to stand. There are, medical men tell me, especial reasons which make this insult galling. Nothing fatigues a woman more than to stand, while a man can stand all day long, and often prefers to transact the whole of his business upon his feet.

As soon as Marcia entered the room Mrs. Huggins sat down in a large easy-chair, and, as she would have said herself, looked the minx over. Marcia on her part waited in silence.

"There are certain things, Miss Conyers," began Mrs. Huggins, "to which I object very strongly. I have been always brought up properly myself, and have been taught to look with disgust upon anything like forwardness or unladylike conduct. Both I and Mr. Huggins" (ego et rex meus) " are disgusted with your conduct. It has really been most disgraceful. I had always understood that your poor father was a perfect gentleman, and that your mother—"

" I will trouble you not to talk about my mother, Mrs. Huggins," said Marcia. " You never knew her."

Here was the opening Mrs. Huggins had wanted. She was on her feet in a moment. When a man wants to tell you that he has had enough of you, but does not care for the trouble of kicking you out, he rings the bell for his lacquey. A woman enters upon a torrent of abuse, spangled with exhortations to you to get out.

"And never wanted to know her either," said Mrs. Huggins. "But if she had lived, poor lady, she would have taught her daughter better. I was not born yesterday, miss. I can see through a brick wall as far as most people, and I consider your conduct a disgrace to a Christian household. A young nobleman in the rank of Lord Norwich has his own friends and his own relations, and I have no doubt you know that well enough. I don't intend to have this house disgraced by any such carryings-on. It's bad enough to have the maid-servants leaving in disgrace, as always will happen when you are near the barracks."

At what precise point is human patience to stop? Marcia was not a man. She could not, for instance, knock Mrs. Huggins down. Neither could she enter into a war of words with her. A sneer or sarcasm would have been wasted. Marcia turned on her heel and walked towards the door.

"Miss Conyers!" called out Mrs. Huggins in a somewhat raised tone of voice, partly as if she were afraid that Marcia was going in quest of some deadly weapon, partly in a tone of command, as if she wished to still further impress the occasion. "Miss Conyers, come back at once. I insist! I order you! Do you hear me, Miss

Conyers?" But Marcia passed through the door, and shut it after her. And Mrs. Huggins, some very naughty words struggling to her lips, subsided into the easy-chair and wept.

Hysterics were unnecessary, as there was no gentleman present, but she had what the ladies'-maid, who surprised her at its conclusion, afterwards described to the other domestics as a real good howl.

Marcia on her part went straight to her room, and packed her two boxes; rang the bell, and ordered that a cab should be sent for; and so was fairly on her way to Fräulein Dietz before Mrs. Huggins had recovered from her first burst of sobbing, and had, as the young athletes of the running-path term it, got her second wind.

The cabman drove to Old Chelsea, where he deposited her and her effects at the door of Fräulein Dietz. He was pleased with his fare, and remarked at the first public-house at which he stopped to "wet" the sum, that he had driven a lady who "*was* a lady." "A spanker," he added solemnly.

Cabmen, to use their own terminology, can "reckon up a fare" pretty accurately. The estimate made by her driver of Marcia was as accurate as had been that one made of her father, and recorded in these pages by a gentleman whose position in life was also "upon the rank."

CHAPTER V.

Now it so happened that the Fräulein was at home when Marcia arrived. When a man is at home and nothing else to do, and nothing to take him out, he lights his pipe and sits down in the window, or if it is winter, similarly lights his pipe and lies down on the sofa. When a woman has nothing else to do she substitutes tea for the masculine pipe, and, according to the time of the day and the condition of the light, either indulges herself in a novel or else knits mechanically.

Fräulein Dietz was sitting before the fireplace. The tea was actually standing upon the table, and there was nothing to be done after Marcia's boxes had been safely dragged into the hall, except to indulge in a good long chat.

The two were old friends, and talked everything out thoroughly—the ultimate conclusion being that old Mrs. Huggins ought to be ashamed of herself, and that as there was actually a bed-room to let in the house, Marcia had better take it for a week at any rate, and see how things went.

This little business satisfactorily arranged, the two friends had a walk along the quaint old road that leads to Fulham, and in their own way were entirely happy. They did a little shopping. Shopping with ladies is a mild form of excitement, and usually a very harmless one. In a way indeed it is positively beneficial, as giving a slight stimulus to trade. Had the two friends been men, they would no doubt have concluded the evening with a brandy-and-soda, and possibly even an hour or a couple of hours at a music-hall.

Marcia and the Fräulein took home a basket of strawberries instead, and soberly discussed them through the long twilight into the hours of gloaming. Over the strawberries the position of affairs was mapped out, and the future of the joint campaign (if an inoffensive partnership in life can so be termed) was definitely settled.

At present there was clearly more than seventy pounds to the good in Marcia's pocket. That would last for some time.

Another picture could be got in hand at once. Little pot-boilers were not to be despised, being like little fish, as sweet as they are small. The Fräulein was not absolutely penniless. Altogether, indeed, the two women had a very cheery prospect before them. For women, happily for themselves and for men too, can live more cheaply than men can, and can economize in a hundred little ways of which men are wholly ignorant. I do not desire to enter into the details of this science of personal economy, but its broad facts must be known to everybody.

Before the two ladies retired for the night there was nothing left to be settled, and each of them, I hope, and have reason to believe, slept the sleep of the just. But the next morning was a busy one.

First of all came the letters Marcia had to write. One was to Mr. Huggins, to tell him how and why she had left his roof, and to thank him for all his past kindness. This epistle, by the Fräulein's advice, was registered, addressed in the most clerkly of hands, and directed to the worthy man's office in the city.

It put Mr. Huggins into a very bad temper. In fact he swore at things in general, and when he got home that evening was by no means so agreeable as his better-half could have wished.

The other letter, a somewhat difficult one, was to Lord Norwich. It was to say that she had left Queen's Gate in consequence of a quarrel with Mrs. Huggins, and was now living with her old governess. She thanked him again for buying her picture; added that she meant to keep hard at her work, and to give all her time to it, and so concluded, not because there was nothing more to be said, but for the very sufficient reason that there was nothing more to be written.

Lord Norwich, when he had finished the letter, locked it up in his desk. "She's as good as gold," he said, as he turned the key; "as true as steel, and as plucky as——" Lord Norwich was not in the habit of writing for general readers, or he might have terminated his sentence with some more refined monosyllable than the one he actually selected. But it was distinctly wrong on his part, and indeed petulant, to waste a few more or less vigorous flowers of speech upon Mrs. Huggins. Which he did.

Now there is in Chelsea a delightful

little street of which I am not going to give the name; but it is well known to city clerks of good position, literary men and artists in a small way, widows, and single ladies of limited means, and other such eligible tenants. I will call it Cherry Tree Walk. It runs as nearly as may be due north and south. There is not a public-house or even a shop in its whole length. All the houses have gardens in the rear, and some of them have even a little patch in front. Others are detached, and boast a poplar or two, or a gnarled elm. Starlings will twitter here under the overhanging eaves, and in summer-time the place is so drowsy, that the whistle of the butcher's boy, as he goes his morning rounds, invades the silence as if it were a very war-whoop.

Here our friends picked a little furnished house, and put it in order, and actually went to the expense of a brass-plate for the garden-gate, with MADAME DIETZ, PROFESSOR OF MUSIC, engraved upon it.

"It looks professional, my dear," said the little woman, "and I am quite old enough to be called Madame, and quite ugly enough too."

It is the first ambition of a young man to live in chambers or lodgings of his own. It is a woman's first ambition to have a house of her own. Her first house is as distinct a step in her existence as years ago were her long skirts, or as is for the schoolboy his own double-barrelled gun.

Where there is a will there are many ways, and Crocus Cottage in a few days became as bright and cheerful and fresh as if the spring flowers had fallen on it, to the exclusion of the rest of the street.

All that was needed was a servant; and when a homely, trustworthy girl had been found, and the policeman had been spoken to, and tradesmen selected and coals laid in, the Fräulein rubbed her hands and vowed that she felt twenty years younger, and exactly like Robinson Crusoe in his island. Her infectious good temper communicated itself to Marcia, and I do not think that any two women were ever happier.

In a very few days Marcia was at work. There are some exquisite little bits of country scenery in Old Chelsea—a fact of which very few Londoners are aware. There are the gardens of the Apothecaries'

Company, which are very quaint, curious, and prim; there are charming little nooks to be found in Battersea Park, which is, to my thinking, the prettiest and most natural park in all London. The river is full of life, and rich in colour, and nothing is more easy than to obtain permission to pitch your easel regularly in some secure and sheltered spot. Or, if you go further afield, all the most beautiful part of Middlesex and Surrey is open to you.

People who go out of London for scenery can hardly know much of the Thames between Old Battersea Bridge and Hampton Court.

And now a very curious little string of events came following each upon the other. Marcia, who had just finished a small picture of barges on the slack tide off the

Crabtree, was astonished by a letter requesting a call, which she received from the eminent gentleman, who, according to his own view of the matter, had made her fortune by discovering at a glance exactly the kind of frame it was that her first picture had needed.

He wanted her, he said, to paint him half-a-dozen small things, all about the same size. She might chose her own subjects. He was in no particular hurry. He would take them as they were done, according to season, opportunity, and so forth. He was commissioned to give the order, and was prepared to state that the price he was willing to offer would be sixty guineas for each picture, provided of course that it was, as it certainly would be, equal to Miss Conyers' rising reputation.

Talk of fortune at once! Why Marcia was fairly bewildered. The news seemed too good to be true. Could it possibly be the case that Mr. Moss was out of his senses, or was playing a joke upon her? And then she recollected that it was Mr. Huggins who had sent her to Moss, to have her Academy picture varnished and framed. But, she argued with herself, it was absurd to suppose that Mr. Huggins could possibly want a sort of small gallery of pictures from her brush, or that he was sufficiently venturesome to risk the wrath of Mrs. Huggins, if such a purchase on his part were discovered.

She was still very ignorant of the world. It did not occur to her that people act from mixed motives, and that if her pictures had not been honestly worth the money, and if Mr. Huggins had not personally taken a sort of kindly interest in her welfare, which was as much due to her good looks as to her skill with the brush, and very largely due to his own secret annoyance and irritation at his wife's bad temper, Mr. Huggins would never have thus loosened his purse-strings.

Here, however, was the order. From whom it came did not so much matter. 'And Marcia set to work upon it in steady earnest.

The days and weeks that followed ran the tranquil course of a mill-stream. Picture after picture was painted, and punctually sent in. The purchase-money was as punctually paid, so that Marcia and the Fräulein were in their little way quite affluent, and became full of small plans and schemes for the future.

It was as well perhaps that this should
be so, for the music-lessons had not exactly
turned out a mine of wealth, and it was
fortunate also that there should be absolutely no ground for anything like forebod-
ings. It is almost impossible to do work
of any kind, still less work of the highest
kind, unless your mind is at ease.

When you are happy, time flies. When
you are busy it flies also. You must look
at your watch if you are out fishing or
shooting and the sport is good, otherwise
you will miss your train, or somehow else
get home inconveniently late. If you are
hard at work, even upon a mathematical
problem, you will be astonished to find
how rapidly the minutes have flown. This
is why busy people are always contented.
It is when time hangs heavy on your

hands that you begin to fret, or, as Homer called it, to gnaw at your soul.

Now the Fräulein was always busy. Her whole life was a little atmosphere of activity. Her mental organization was that of a coral reef, which is always ceaselessly at work, until line by line, and inch by inch, it has grown into an island. Marcia's energy was more concentrated and intense. And so at last, when the Fräulein came in one evening from some small purchases, she was astonished to be pounced upon by Marcia, who seized her by her two shoulders, ran her up to the easel, and called out with a loud laugh, "There's the last! It must go in to-morrow morning."

"And then?" asked the Fräulein.

"The picture goes in, and we go off."

The Fräulein collapsed into a chair. "Where to?" she gasped.

"Anywhere! anywhere! anywhere!" trilled Marcia. "Pegwell Bay, Athens, Scarborough, St. Petersburg, Malvern, Memphis. Where you please."

"Dieppe is a nice place I have heard," said the Fräulein, "and very healthy."

"We will start to-morrow," said Marcia, "and leave the picture on our way to the station." And this they actually did. For Marcia was not a fussy young lady. She rather resembled Lord Clyde, who when asked how soon he would be ready to start for India and quell the mutiny if he could, replied that he should be ready that afternoon.

The Fräulein, on the other hand, was a marvel of neatness and precision—qualities that save time—and would have made a most admirable courier, had she been suddenly called upon to fill such a post at a moment's notice. And so within a very few hours the last picture had been handed to Mr. Moss, a sergeant of police with a responsible wife was in charge of the house, and Marcia and the Fräulein were listening to the dull measured beat of the paddles, as the vessel steamed out into the Channel, and began to feel the tide.

It was for each of them a most delightful change. There is nothing more pleasant for a short time, at any rate, than the methodical activity and busy regularity of a well-managed passenger steamer. There are drawbacks, of course. There is a smell of grease from the engines. There are passengers whose misery cannot escape your notice, and make you feel as if your own comfort and pleasure were somehow a selfish thing, and almost partaking of the nature of sin. It may rain violently, or you may for some other reason be confined below deck against your will.

None of these things, however, troubled either Marcia or her companion. They were in fact almost sorry when the time came for the disembarkment, and the scrutiny of their baggage.

CHAPTER VI.

AND it is now getting time that I should return to John Douglas, who, when we last took leave of him, was not without reason in an extremely touchy state of temper, from the effects of which Marcia's little letter of thanks for his most kindly and apt present had by no means wholly relieved him.

He settled down to his work, of course. He was a giant at work. It did him good. There are some men who are never really happy or at ease unless they are hard at work. They enjoy a short holiday and are the better for it, exactly as they enjoy their sleep and rise from it refreshed. But to keep them in health, whether of mind or of body, they require continuous and severe employment. There are a few such men among the ranks of our aristocracy. Some of them administer their own estates with remarkable skill and success. Others—these are few—take to science or to travel. There are many men in the army who are there simply because soldiering gives them something to do.

The career of a successful barrister from the Quarter Sessions to the Woolsack does not, as a rule, especially if it be at all truthful, afford pleasant or edifying matter for a biography. In the lives of the Chancellors and of the Lord Chief Justices of England, there is much to make us sad. We find miserable little intrigues and jealousies, and as the history advances a process of gradual hardening or ossification going on in the man's heart.

Even if Campbell was unjust to his rivals, as it is pretty certain he was, we may make a large allowance for his spitefulness and vanity, and shall still not find the picture a pleasant one.

And John Douglas was no exception to a rule under which greater and abler and better men than himself have been included. He became hardened. He lost wholesome pleasure in wholesome enjoyments to which he had once been attached. He practically gave up field sports, not because he was too old for them, or felt his eye growing dim and his nerve failing him, but because he was, without knowing it, becoming fossilized.

Nobody was surprised when he applied for silk and got it, or when, as a mechanical matter of course, he employed a Parliamentary agent in Finsbury Circus, who for a given price found him an eligible constituency, or when after a year or two—not more—he became Sir John Douglas and Solicitor-General. It was all matter of course.

Men envied him his success, but nobody suggested for a moment that it was not thoroughly deserved.

As for the Oakshire episode in his life, it remained in his memory, as did everything else that had ever had a place there. But beyond a memory it was nothing to him. He neither kept it fondly alive nor strove to banish it. It was among the things that had been, and there was an end of it.

One of our greatest Chancellors once visited a cathedral town. He took with him to the afternoon service a young barrister, and specially directed his young friend's attention to a somewhat corpulent lay clerk with a tenor voice distinctly past its prime. "That man," said he, as he left the precincts with his companion, " I once envied more than any other human being in the world. There was a vacancy among the choristers. I was a candidate, and so was he. He was selected. I believe he is a sensible man. If so, and he knew everything, he perhaps would not be anxious after all to change places with me."

A very shrewd old Baron of the Exchequer in the good old days expressed a similar opinion. He was walking down the street at York, when the coach with its four horses was pulled up, in the most approved fashion, at the inn-door, and the driver with proper dignity threw his reins to an ostler and leisurely dismounted.

"He's a happy man," said his Lordship emphatically; "nobody dare contradict him. Now look at me. I have to take my seat on the Bench, and have every young whipper-snapper from Quarter Sessions putting me right. I'm sick of it."

Like the Chancellor, John Douglas wondered at his old self and his own past hopes and wishes. Like the learned Baron he was thoroughly dissatisfied with his position.

Sir Hugo, like all selfish people, had

worked more mischief than he ever dreamed of, and had utterly spoilt not John Douglas' success in life as measured by any ordinary standard, but his life itself. The story is not a new one. Such things happen every day, and Providence still permits wretched meddlers such as Sir Hugo to make the world miserable in the pursuit of their own petty purposes.

We must console ourselves if we can with the assurance that all things work together for good. But this is a belief that requires a sturdy faith.

"The good man," says Plato, "will be happy even whilst he is being broken on the wheel." "People who tell us this kind of thing," is the trenchant criticism of his greatest pupil, the sage of Stagira, "may mean what they say, or may not.

But in either case they are talking non-
sense." The remark was unkindly as from
a pupil towards his old teacher. But it
was the perfection of philosophy, which is
only the perfection of common sense.

No man can be happy who is suffering the
slow torture of discontent. And no discontent is worse than that which arises when
you look back upon a fatal mistake which
has robbed your life of its sunshine. You
cannot cheat your own soul by telling yourself that, after all, you have done very
well.

Napoleon did very well after he divorced
Josephine. But I often fancy he must have
been haunted by her memory even when
his star seemed to himself and to all Europe
at its highest.

Sir John Douglas married, of course.

The marriage was a most prudent one. People called it an admirable match. The lady was the second daughter of a Law Lord. She was considered handsome; she had considerable natural ability, which in its way had been improved by education, and she had thirty thousand pounds. She had also a strong will, and could hold her own. Douglas was no prodigy in her eyes, and he very soon became aware of the fact.

Many a man has been spoilt beyond hope by the over-worship of his wife. But on the whole such a fate is happier than that of the man whose wife gives him plainly to understand that in her opinion their union has been a most suitable one, and from its practical aspect a remarkably good thing for him. Consequently John Douglas chafed, and was happiest perhaps when dining alone at the Athenæum, or preparing in his study an argument which would afterwards, he knew, be quoted as of quasi-judicial authority. His life was dull. Sympathy had no longer an existence for him.

"Life," said Heraclitus of Ephesus, "is no better than death."

"Then why do you live on?" asked a busybody.

"Because," said Heraclitus, "death is no better than life."

And in this frozen frame of mind Sir John Douglas lived on.

Now if it had not been for the meddlesome and wholly selfish manœuvring of Sir Hugo, Douglas would almost certainly have married our heroine, and it is almost equally certain that the marriage would have ended in that solid happiness which after all is the best. Marriages of affection pure and simple are all very well in their way. I have nothing to say against them, and I suppose they will continue till the end of time. But marriages of good sound common sense combined with that particular kind of affection that deepens later in life into regard and respect of the highest kind, are the best of all—best in their inception, and best in their results.

That Marcia did not become the wife of John Douglas was entirely the fault of Sir Hugo, and if we look about us we shall find that nearly all the unhappiness in this world is brought upon people, not through their own selfishness, but through the selfishness of others, and more especially of their own relations.

What had Sir Hugo, for instance, ever done for Marcia to give him the slightest claim upon her gratitude, or to warrant him for a moment in attempting to control the course of her life for his own selfish purposes? Every day we see girls sacrificed hopelessly in this manner. Every day relations interfere in matters upon which they have really no moral right to express an opinion. We laugh in England at the idea of the French *conseil de famille;* but it equally exists among ourselves, although it is not formally recognized by the law.

And the lives of those who have allowed this kind of shoddy destiny to influence their career, or who have been powerless to prevent its doing so, are too frequently wasted lives in the most unhappy sense of the term.

The worst of one's relations is that they hardly make the pretence of being disinterested. They talk to you, for instance, about what you owe to your family. Now let any man ask himself why young Smith, who wants to be a surgeon and has a distinct genius that way, owes it to his family that he should go into the Church? Why does his sister owe it to her family that she should marry the banker in her county town whom she personally dislikes, and not the young officer to whom she is really attached, and who is anxious for her sake to exchange into a regiment in India?

In one of Dickens' greatest works, Mrs. Merdle, the wife of the supposed millionnaire, tells him sharply that he does not sufficiently consider his duty to society. Mr. Merdle's reply is to the effect, that for years past he has turned himself into a watering-pot, and watered society with gold; and, he adds, he should much like to know what society has ever done for him.

Let any man in his quiet and sound moments ask himself how much he really owes to his relations. He will find, nine times out of ten, that if anything has been done for him, it has been done by his friends—friends whom he has made for himself entirely without the aid of his family, and, as a rule, directly against the advice of its responsible members.

We are often told that a man's worst enemy is himself. On the contrary, a man's worst foes are those of his own household. Leave him to make his own bed, and you will find him quite content to lie upon it. He will not come round with his hat in his hand, unless it be for some absolutely justifiable reason which would give him a claim upon the compassion even of perfect strangers. But we take young people, and play at Providence with them as a child plays at Providence with its dolls. If the result is a moderate humdrum success, we claim the credit. If it be a failure, we ostentatiously wash our hands of the matter, and loudly disclaim our responsibility.

It is considered the proudest jewel upon the matron's brow that she should have married all her daughters well. Notice the phrase, my reader, and analyse it. It is not that she has married them happily, but that she has married them well, which is quite another thing. The

phrase also is that she has married them—
as if the matter were one in which they
themselves had no voice. In the same
way we might put it among the qualifications of a gardener, that he was a
remarkably clever potter and bedder-out.
But plants are mechanical things, more or
less. Human beings are not. Certainly
there was nothing mechanical about Marcia.
And yet here was old Sir Hugo pottering
about with his little flower-pot, and his
little potful of loam, and his wretched
little empirical views as to temperature,
and other essential conditions of healthy
plant life. Your gardener does not care
for the plant itself a whiff of the coarse
tobacco that he burns in your hot-houses
to kill insects. What he wants is to take
a prize at the next county flower-show.

So Sir Hugo, having no other seedling available for his purposes but Marcia, had made up his mind that she should win a prize for him.

He is not the first excellent and wholly unselfish man who has been suddenly snatched away from us before he has had time to complete his good work. Perhaps in a larger sphere of existence, there may be more for us to do than to play at Providence on our own account. After all, Sir Hugo was a very respectable old offender. He was no worse than many other men of his own stamp, and better than some. If he had succeeded in marrying his daughter to Lord Norwich, the matrons from the poorer districts would certainly not have assembled at the doors of the sacred edifice to hoot and yell at him as he left the church—a thing that actually happened to a lady of title in this most Christian country, within the memory of most of my readers. He was, after all, a lazy, indolent old sinner, who, if all his own wishes were first fully satisfied, would probably rather have seen other people round about him happy than not.

This is negative praise; but as far as it goes it may be given ungrudgingly.

CHAPTER VII.

OUT of the Grand Rue in Dieppe a number of little streets trickle down, as it were, to the sea. One of them is the Rue Champsfleuris. At its seaward extremity it is flanked on the right hand by the wide wall of an enormous hotel and pension, and on the opposite side by the wall of a large English boarding-school for young ladies. Above these are little shops where they sell charcoal and sausages and bread, and other such small merchandise. The only shop of note in the street sells bibles, breviaries, rosaries of olive wood from Gethsemane, book-markers, and Lives of the Saints, while in its window is a crucifix certified to contain a fragment of the *vera crux*. Here Marcia and the Fräulein took up their abode.

They got, at a most reasonable rental, a small room on the *entresol*, and a bedroom above it. And when they had arranged that they were to take all their meals out, with the exception of tea, there was literally nothing left to be done, except to saunter about the decayed old town, and look at the cathedral and the flower-market and the beach.

Dieppe is for such English as frequent it a city of the lotos-eaters. They do nothing, and find their happiness in doing it thoroughly. In the season, no doubt,

Americans, and English, and even a certain number of Parisians come to Dieppe to bathe and to enjoy themselves in their own way. Indeed, after the races at Deauville, there is a regular exodus towards the town. The sun shines, and the thrifty people of Dieppe make their money. So in England, during a very brief period of our summer, even Broadstairs blossoms into life. But out of the season, Dieppe is the sort of place a man would select in which to live cheaply and exactly as he pleased, to write a book, or make an attempt to write one, to avoid harsh and importunate creditors, and generally for reasons bad, indifferent or good, to bury himself.

To enjoy Dieppe at all out of the season, you must be much such a philosopher as Gilbert White. I doubt, indeed, if even that most estimable of English scholars, naturalists, and parsons would have been fully equal to Dieppe and its worthy inhabitants during the autumnal equinox.

It was now, however, August, and Dieppe was as lively as is Cowes in the regatta month. Had Marcia kept a diary, her entries would have been amusing. The Frenchwomen, especially the Parisians, were an inexhaustible source of enjoyment to her. The Frenchmen amused her almost as much. The children in their fancy costumes were a constant study. The English were of that particular English type which affects Dieppe and Boulogne, and asserts itself by doing as it pleases, in its most obtrusive and offensive manner. So much for Dieppe itself.

But a little inland, amid the most exquisite Norman scenery, lies Arques, and
it was at Arques that Marcia, accompanied
by the Fräulein, spent the best part of
every day. The young lady set to work
methodically. She devoted an entire week
to studying the scenery, until she had
thoroughly got herself into sympathy with
its character, and mastered its moods of
colour and changes of expression. Then
after much strategy in the choice of a
situation she set to work upon her new
picture.

The Château d'Arques is one that grows
upon you. It will make the pursiest
stockbroker out of Throgmorton Street
feel a sort of twinge of romance to wander
under the old walls, and think vaguely
of their history, and of the stories they

could tell if they chose, and which would be far more wonderful than those that the *gardien* so glibly pours into the ears of the excursionists to the famous Château. Where the red tomatoes now ripen under the wall, and the ducks and poultry roam unmolested, men in armour once strode heavily to and fro. The empty courtyards were once busy with life. The chambers of state had their stone panelled with oak, which in its own turn was hidden from the eye by rich, heavily-broidered tapestry. To do the ruins of a castle justice, you must in your own mind clothe the dry bones with flesh. And to do this task Marcia's imagination was fully equal. For, indeed, the most resolute minds have as much imagination as have others, and occasionally even more. And it was in this spirit that she set to work upon her picture.

All the elements of success were at last combined. She was not working under any kind of pressure, or even against time. She could do her work in her own way, and according to her own humour, commencing it, discontinuing it, and resuming it, as she pleased. The task was congenial, and more than itself lay in the future beyond it. And above all it was voluntary.

The life of an artist is self-chosen. He is not brought up to it as are bankers, or merchants, or the bulk of business and professional men. Very few artists paint for the sake of money alone. Even Turner, when engaged upon his pictures, and not in bargaining about their price, must have had his happy moments. Marcia herself was probably never so happy as at this particular juncture.

But there is one little point I must not forget, as it lets a light on my heroine's character. Directly, she had profited by her dealings with Mr. Moss, and indirectly, by his stray crumbs of wisdom. So when the day was not favourable for the great work itself, which was seldom, or when Marcia did not feel in the full vein for it, which was still more seldom, she would occupy herself—I am bound to use the only word open to me—with a little pot-boiler. These pot-boilers go by a bigger title. They are called Studies. Their place in the work of the artist is very much that of scales in the education of the musician. But the musician of eminence does not play the scales in public, and as lawyers would say, for reward in that behalf. He plays them in the solitude of his own room.

Now the studies of an artist, if they find their way into the market, have an appreciable value. An educated taste for Art is far more frequent than a purse of sufficient length to gratify it. But a small picture even unfinished will always command its price, if the painter be well known. Men of mark do not usually sell these things themselves. But their executors do. Men who are not yet recognized as being in the first rank find the pot-boiler a most useful and aptly-named product of their labour. And so, with unceasing industry, the moments in which justice could not be adequately done to the great work itself, were devoted to the manufacture of these most useful and sensible trifles. I may dismiss them by saying that they considerably more than covered all the expenses of the visit to Dieppe, and that five years afterwards they were worth at a public auction prices which to Marcia when she was engaged upon them would have seemed fabulous.

Now while the picture was occupying the hours and the pot-boilers were filling up the moments, a schooner, with the white flag of the Royal Yacht Squadron, threw anchor one night off Dieppe, and next morning at high tide was towed into the harbour. She was of English build, with sails by Lapthorne, with a deck-house of plate-glass, and with that marvellous neatness and completeness in every arrangement which serves to remind us how wise Socrates must have been.

Whenever, said Socrates, a man gives his mind to a thing, he does it better than any woman can. Let us take two arts in which women are supposed to employ themselves more especially than in others—cookery and millinery. In each of these men drive them hopelessly out of the field. Now if there is one thing upon which women are supposed to pride themselves more than another it is upon the neatness and beauty of their homes, and more especially of the state chambers. But there is not a boudoir in the world to compare for a moment with the saloon of a yacht that carries a competent steward, nor can any house show a floor equal to a properly holy-stoned deck.

All Dieppe turned out to have a look at the vessel, and of course everybody knew all about her. She belonged to a rich American, who had brought her over from New York to challenge all our English yachtsmen. She was the summer whim of a Russian Grand Duke, and her saloon was an Aladdin's palace. She had been built in San Francisco for a gentleman who had struck oil, and who had brought her across the Pacific through the China Seas and round the Cape of Good Hope, past Gibraltar, and up into the Mediterranean, from whence he was on his way to the English coast, and so to Christiania.

The vessel herself was so exquisite in her lines, so admirably found, so beautiful and complete down to the smallest detail, that none of these conjectures was extravagant

in itself, though all were wide of the mark.
She was the 'Cecilia' of the Royal Yacht
Squadron, as the harbour-master could have
told these speculators, and she had just
brought Lord Norwich over from Cowes.

Lord Norwich himself—only they did
not know him by sight—was comfortably
reclining in a deck-chair close by the main
hatchway, and occupied with a French novel
and a Havannah cigar. He was dressed as
an English yachtsman ought to be—that
is to say, you would have passed him in
the street without noticing anything pro-
nouncedly nautical in his costume.

Frenchmen soon get tired of looking at
anything, and the crowd round the yacht
melted away. Lord Norwich, indifferent
to the interest taken in his vessel and
himself, was pulled in the cutter to the

landing-place, and thence sauntered leisurely up into the town. It was no mere whim had brought him to Dieppe. He had ascertained with some little trouble that Marcia and the Fräulein had gone there. "I may as well take a run to Dieppe as to anywhere else," he said. "I would sooner go to Dieppe than to any other place in the world," was what he really thought. "It's a beastly hole," said some of his friends. "So are most places," answered his Lordship, "and I needn't stop unless I like."

As for his steward and his sailing-master they thought nothing. Sailors occasionally assume a meditative air, but it is extremely doubtful whether they ever think.

Lord Norwich had a look along the *Plage*, but Marcia was not there. He explored the somewhat dreary stretch of beach with his

binocular, but in vain. Then he thought
he would try the Casino. " As likely to be
there as anywhere else," he said. So into
the Casino he went. There was no concert
going on at the moment, neither was there
any bathing, as it was either the wrong time
of day, or the wrong time of the tide, or
perhaps both. Neither was Marcia playing
at the *Petits Chévaux* (the proprietors of
which amusing game of chance were driving
an uncommonly brisk trade), nor eating ices,
nor knitting. She was not in the *salon de
lecture*, which was dolefully empty. But he
found her at last under the awning, where
she was seated with the Fräulein, and most
contentedly doing nothing.

As soon as he saw her, Lord Norwich
took off his straw hat and stood still. Now,
whatever you are doing, if any one walks

up towards you and suddenly stands still you are bound to look up. Marcia looked up, and at once broke into a pleasant smile. There was no reason on earth why she should not do so. Then, of course, they shook hands, and then the Fräulein had to be introduced. Lord Norwich, standing easily by them—it is only an Englishman who can stand naturally—began to talk about everything and nothing.

He commenced with a tremendous falsehood, that he had come to Dieppe in his yacht entirely by accident. Then he became violently interested in Arques. He must go over with them if they would let him, and have a look at the place. He had heard of it, of course. It had something to do with Joan of Arc, he believed. No doubt Miss Dietz would put him right if he was wrong. Fräulein Dietz was not quite sure, but she knew that it was a very beautiful castle, and she for her own part preferred it to Pembroke or even to Kenilworth, both of which Lord Norwich no doubt had seen.

Then they got talking about Glastonbury Abbey and the swans, and Furness Abbey where the deadly nightshade grows, and Lord Norwich said that it was one of the few places in England where that sinister-looking plant is to be found. And then when it had been settled that Lord Norwich was to go over with them next day to Arques, it was also arranged that the day after, if it were fine, they should take a run in the 'Cecilia' along the coast. Both Marcia and the Fräulein were charmed with this idea, each of them having misty notions of the yacht, and believing it to contain unheard-of splendours and luxuries.

Then they began to talk about the Huggins. Lord Norwich, in his blunt way, was very glad that Marcia had left Queen's Gate. Marcia owned that her life with them had at the last become intolerable, but was careful to put in a kind word for the head of the household, and frankly told the story of how much she owed the warm-hearted old stockbroker; and how, if it had not been for him, she would not now have been in France.

Lord Norwich profoundly observed that city men were very often uncommonly good fellows, and that he himself enjoyed a city dinner immensely, always excepting the Mansion House itself, where the cookery was atrocious. He had dined once with the

Goldsmiths, not at one of their big dinners, but at a select gathering of the Warden, the Vice-Warden, the Prime Wardens, and their friends; and the plate was actually triple gilt, and a good deal of it solid gold. As for the amount they spent in charity it was a dozen times what they spent in entertainments, and for the life of him he failed to see why the Radicals could not let them alone.

As for Mr. Huggins, he intended as soon as he returned to England to improve his acquaintance. With regard to Mrs. Huggins he could only say that he was sorry for her husband, who worked hard when he did work, and deserved a better time of it when he got home. Then the Huggins family dropped out of the conversation, and before long they all three found themselves sauntering down to the harbour.

When they reached that part of the quay where the 'Cecilia' was lying, Marcia and the Fräulein had a succession of astonishments. There is nothing so bewildering to any one who sees it for the first time as the exquisite order and dainty perfection of a yacht in which its owner takes a pride, and can afford to gratify his whim.

The little gangway was thrown out, and they found themselves on a deck which had that morning been religiously holystoned till it shone like polished parquet. The sails and ropes were faultlessly clean, the masts had just been scraped, and the funnel repainted. The brass nails and the binnacle were as perfectly in order as if

they were costly instruments from an
optician's window. There was a small
deck cargo of coal in white canvas sacks,
with leather straps and handles. There
was the deck-house with its plate-glass
windows and velvet fittings and spring-
blinds.

Then, of course, they had to see the
saloon, and to look down the companion
into the engine-room, where they could
see machinery as scrupulously clean as if
it were part of some gigantic watch which
a grain of dust might throw out of gear.
On the deck were the delightful P. and
O. lounges with their arms doing duty for
small tables. The wheel was covered up
in white canvas. All round it, and upon
the roof of the deck-house, and here and
there on stands against the bulwarks, the

sailing-master had ranged flowers in pots; bright red geraniums contrasted with the yellow calceolaria, and the deliciously-scented heliotrope.

They went forward to inspect the windlass, and when they turned and found their way back to the deck-house, the steward, radiant in navy blue, gilt buttons, and white waistcoat, stood at the door wherein he had arranged a little banquet that might have satisfied the censorship of Bignon himself—hot-house fruits, prawns, potted meats, champagne in ice, quaint sweetmeats, and in the centre of the small table an ingenious fountain that spirted up a tiny jet of rosewater into a basin filled with cut flowers.

It is a solemn fact, but not to my mind at all a painful or even an unpleasant one,

M 2

that women, especially the kind of women whom men like and who deserve that men should like them, are as fond of the nice things of this world as is an Eton school-boy, or even an ecclesiastical dignitary of high position. I could give reasons for this. Men always celebrate a big occasion with a big feed. When they make a *coup* they usually invite their friends to dinner. But a big dinner for itself, and without an occasion to give it sufficient reason, bores them.

At the best clubs in London men who can afford themselves every luxury habitually dine off a little soup and fish, the joint of the house, with mashed potatoes and a pint of wine. If Lord Steyne or Mr. Goldmore the banker were to go into one of his clubs and order himself a dinner of four or five courses, the waiters would mention the matter to one another, and would all wonder whether anything had gone wrong with him.

But a woman is *gourmet* by her very nature. Adam would never have wanted anything better than a plain potato. It was Eve who beguiled him with Ribston pippins. Marcia and the Fräulein were true women after all, and the steward of the 'Cecilia' felt a proud man when he saw how his efforts were appreciated.

Lunch and ices over there was a new surprise. For instead of the gangway being run out to the pier, a companion was lowered on the waterside, and at her foot lay the long-boat, with four blue-jackets on the thwarts and the sailing-master in the stern-sheets.

The boat herself was as marvellously

complete as the yacht, and in her they
shot with a quick stroke out of the harbour-
mouth, past the lighthouse and round the
pier, and so dashed along the shore until
they reached the Casino itself. The crew
of the 'Cecilia' were picked men, and the
little craft darted through the water and
brought up at the Casino with that finish,
down to the minutest detail, which is the
perfection of seamanship.

"So that is Lord Norwich," said the
Fräulein to Marcia, when that young nobleman had bade them good-bye at their door.
"So that is Lord Norwich. Well, I can only
say that I have the best opinion of him, and
that I cannot congratulate you, my dear
Marcia, upon the way you have treated him."

"He has no reason to complain of any
ill-treatment upon my part, Fräulein Dietz."

"Perhaps not. But can't you see how he loves you? Why, my dear, that man would go to his death for you. Surely he deserves something in return."

"I wish you would not talk about it, Fräulein. It is not an agreeable subject to me. I am very sorry for Lord Norwich if he has set his mind upon me. I do not, however, think that at all likely. As I told you, we had a thorough understanding at St. Austell's Towers, and I am confident that he regards the matter in the same light as I do."

"And I am confident that he does not."

"If you are right, Fräulein, it is not my fault. I cannot help it if I am unable to reciprocate his affection. You would not have me marry without caring for him. That is, without caring for him as I ought to. And I hate the idea of marriage. I don't want to marry any one."

"You are an extraordinary girl, Marcia. Why, that man would make your life one delirium of happiness. He is young, he is noble, he is honest, and he is rich. What in heaven's name more do you want?"

"You don't understand, my dear Fräulein."

"No, my dear, I do not."

CHAPTER VIII.

Early next morning they started for Arques. Lord Norwich had a habit aptly described by vulgar Englishmen in a phrase of three words. He liked to do things well. Aristotle, in the profoundest treatise on moral philosophy that the world has ever yet had from an uninspired pen, exalts this art of doing things well, or as they ought to be done, to the rank of a high moral virtue.

If you are a poor man, he says, you had better not ask your friends to dinner at all.

They will quite understand your apparent negligence, and sympathize with you. But if you are to ask them to dinner, you must give them an entertainment that does credit to yourself, and is a compliment to them.

If you overdo the thing, you are purse-proud. If you attempt it and fail, you are a snob, like Thackeray's poor dear Major Ponto. You must take the middle course —the *auria mediocritas* of Horace.

Lord Norwich was a gentleman—which is much better than being a nobleman. He hunted all over Dieppe, and actually got together a very serviceable team of Normandy greys and a presentable English coach. Inside he stowed the lunch, or rather had it stowed. On the back-seats were his steward and one or two of the

crew held deserving of an outing. You
can never have too many sailors about you.
Apparently the most indolent of men, they
are in reality the most brisk and active.

Marcia and Lord Norwich had the box.
Behind them was the Fräulein with the
yacht's captain, who respectfully perched
himself at the extreme edge of the seat,
where he sat in silence with his feet hanging over the road, and looking for all the
world like a mast-headed middy of somewhat advanced age.

Dieppe turned out to see the English
Milord who steered his own yacht, and
could drive his own four-in-hand. The
Normandy people are sympathetic. It does
them good to see others happy. The
veterans among them did not quite approve
of the start. They had expected that Lord

Norwich would distribute a few oaths all
round as from an *arrosoir*, crack his whip
till he woke the echoes, and start at a full
gallop.

Instead of all this he started at a slow
trot, keeping his team well together. So
they voted the thing tame, and sagely remarked to one another that he did not take
a proper pride in himself. It is a pretty
journey from Dieppe to Arques. Probably
most of my readers know it. They rattled
along past rich meadows where the cattle
stood knee-deep in grass, and over quaint
bridges beneath which trout-streams pleasantly rippled ; and the villagers turned
out to look at them, and the men at work
by the road-side and in the fields shaded
their eyes with their hands, and stopped
to gaze ; and so at last they clattered

merrily into Arques itself, and pulled up
in the most approved fashion before the
leading inn in that historical village.

The horses were taken out, and the little
village crowd dispersed. Then came lunch,
and after lunch was over, Marcia, accompanied by Lord Norwich and the Fräulein,
proceeded at once to her usual position,
and, without a moment's delay, recom-
menced her work. The Fräulein produced
some complicated knitting. Lord Norwich
thrust his .hands into his pockets and
looked on.

Now it so happened that on that particular day the sun had, as on every other
day, its accustomed apparent motion. The
Fräulein, whose blood had circulated more
quickly when she was younger. shifted her
position with the sun, and at last was fairly

out of ear-shot. Marcia went on painting. Lord Norwich went on looking over her shoulder.

It was a lovely day ; but his lordship did did not seem to feel his way to say as much. The picture was a remarkably good one. But then if he had ventured on that observation it would have looked as if he were paying the ordinary stereotyped compliment. Of painting in its technicalities he was as profoundly ignorant as of cat's-cradle or the differential calculus. At last, however, to tell the story in his own words, he began to pull himself together.

" I think I shall like this picture, Miss Conyers, even better than your Academy one. May I ask permission, so to say, to become the owner of it now ? "

" Of course you may, if you like. But

I must finish it first. And then I must ask you to let it be exhibited. And we must be horribly mercenary over the matter, and get somebody to fix the proper price for us—somebody who doesn't care a bit one way or the other, but will give us what is called the auction value. You see I am getting learned in all the minor mysteries of my art. I suppose some hundred or so views of Arques are painted every season, and mine will be one among them."

Then she stopped and laughed. "I won't sell it at all, Lord Norwich. I will be as obstinate as that vicious old Turner, or that horrible Sibyl with her books. Let me finish the picture in my own way, and you shall have it. I like it. I have been very happy over it for many hours, and I simply refuse to sell it at all."

And then she began to fill in some clusters of wallflower and stock on one of the crumbling towers. This little work of detail required a number of colours, so that she had to consult her palette very closely.

Lord Norwich was silent for a minute. He looked at the picture. Then he looked at his boots. Apparently he found some inspiration in them, for he drew a long breath and began to speak.

"I wish you would give me the picture, Miss Conyers. You would make me just the very happiest man in the world. Only what I want is—I mean I wish—that is to say, I want you to give me something else along with it. I don't want to give you pain, or even to trouble you. I know what worry you must have had these last few months. And I am afraid that I am troubling you. I would sooner be off at once for the North Pole, or the Fiji Islands. But do let me ask you to give me the picture and yourself as well. I can't say anything more, and it's very difficult to say this. But if you could only just give me the idea that I had some sort of a chance—only a chance—I would wait any time. It's no use writing about these kind of things. Can't you tell me that there is some kind of hope for me? I shall be content if it is ever so indistinct. Say 'hat, and I will stop here, or I will go away, or I will do anything you tell me to do. I feel it's no good going on. But I do assure you, Miss Conyers, you can make me. I could do something worth doing with you to guide me, and up to now I can't help feeling that my life has been wasted. I have had heaps of opportunities, and I have nothing to show for them. But I could try to be worthy of you, and I would try, with all my heart and soul."

Marcia laid down her brush, which until now she had kept in her hand, and clasped her knees. Then, after a few seconds of silence, she found words.

"I cannot do what you ask me, Lord Norwich; it would not be right. Nor would it be fair to you if I did. I never had a brother, and you seem to me, and always have seemed, more like a brother than anything else. But I cannot say more than that. The world is large, and time is long. There are some things that are secrets to oneself. I cannot tell you my secrets. They are not many. But I do not mind telling you what I expect to do.

I mean to go on quietly with my work, exactly as if nothing had ever passed between us. And I am very, very grateful to you, because I know you have been speaking the truth. And if ever it lays in my poor power to show my gratitude, rest assured that you will not find me unmindful of all your kindness. I shall always look on you and on my dear Fräulein as my two best friends—indeed almost my only friends. For I am not likely to make others. Look! The sun is setting, and the colours are all becoming purple grey. You must help me to pack up, Lord Norwich. There is nothing more to be done to-day, or said."

So they packed up, and the easel and painting implements, and the picture itself, securely fastened into the deal-box, were deposited for the night with the old lady at the castle, who acted as their custodian; and then they strolled down the hill into the village.

At the door of the little inn the horses were tossing their heads and pawing their feet in anxiety to get back; and it was hardly a minute before they were rattling merrily along the really beautiful road.

Lord Norwich drove his best, and the great iron-grey Normandy horses, although unaccustomed to the touch of an English hand, felt at once they had got their master. At Marcia's door all three got down, and there was a minute or two devoted to the interchange of pleasant farewells. Then the vehicle lumbered off to its stables, the two women with a final shake of the hand went into their house, and Lord Norwich pausing to light a cigar strode down towards the Hôtel Royal.

He scarcely tasted a morsel of the excellent dinner provided for him at that establishment, and paying his bill made his way to the harbour. On board the yacht he impatiently threw off his clothes and tumbled into his cot. The cabin-lamp shed a soft mellow light over the chamber, and everything was hushed except the slight splash of the water in the harbour. Now and then some one from shore would hail a vessel, or the silence would be broken by the shriek of a gull soaring overhead, or by the measured pulse of oars. But beyond this all was still, and Lord Norwich lay in his cot and occupied himself with thinking things over.

Certainly Marcia did not dislike him. That,

his own common sense could tell him without any vanity. He was equally sure that she perfectly believed all he had said. If so, then why on earth should she not marry him? And the more he considered this question, the more difficult he found it to arrive at any practical and satisfactory solution of it.

Nine men out of ten would have resolved to give the whole matter up then and there, and to let the young lady go her own way. Lord Norwich happened to be the tenth man, and he made up his mind to see the thing out, and he knew thoroughly what it all meant. But he determined to choose his own time, and he fully decided to leave Dieppe at once.

All Englishmen are obstinate, and he was, most certainly, no exception to the general rule. " There is time to spare anyhow," he said to himself, "and there is a good deal of virtue in time. 'Time and I against any two,' Napoleon used to say. We will see what the old gentleman can do for me. There is no other fellow in the case, I am sure. If there is, why should she not marry him at once? And if there is no one else, my chance may very likely get the better for a little keeping. At all events the prize is worth a waiting game." And this concise summary of the situation his lordship emphasized with a little strong language, after which he turned round in his cot and fell asleep as soundly as any young man need.

Marcia, on her part, had a few words—actually a few words—with the Fräulein. That excellent lady thought Marcia very foolish, obstinate, and full of false pride, and did not scruple to tell her so. Marcia was of opinion that the matter was one in which she had a right to judge for herself. The Fräulein opined that nobody was infallible in this world, and that it was always better to listen to reason. Marcia retorted that she intended to live her own life, that she would not sacrifice it for anybody, that she had considerable respect for Lord Norwich; but that things were best as they were, and that the world as a whole would get on a deal better if people would not take it upon themselves to interfere with the affairs of others, and attempt to guide their destinies when they were wholly inadequate to the task.

The Fräulein, with the most aggravating assumption of weakness, replied that she had not the least intention for a moment of presuming to play the part of Providence to Marcia, who no doubt was perfectly equal to the task of managing her own affairs. It was Lord Norwich in which the Fräulein was interested; he was very good; he was very warm-hearted; he was thoroughly sincere. He was just, fearless, generous, good-natured almost to a fault, and she was sorry for him.

"You plead his cause so eloquently, my dear Fräulein," Marcia snapped out, "that it is a pity you do not marry him yourself."

This of course was rude and wrong. Fräulein Dietz took up her candle and lit it.

"I repeat, Marcia, that you are not yourself in this matter. For the first time in my life I see you thinking nothing of

other people. The happiness of Lord
Norwich is just as important a matter as
is your own, and you have no right whatever to treat it lightly or recklessly. I
shall begin to think that after all you want
to pivot the world round yourself; and I
should be very sorry to have to believe
that of you."

Having discharged this volley, the Fräulein felt her courage fail her, and she made
a precipitate retreat to her own room.

Marcia was actually too tired with all
that had taken place in the day to indulge
herself with any more thinking. " It is no
good," she said to herself, " turning matters
over when you have thoroughly made up
your own mind." And with this reflection
she blew out her candle.

The reflection was a sound one, so far

as it went. But, like all such general state-
ments, it needed modification. For, in
the first place, it was extremely doubtful
whether Marcia really had made up her
mind, or whether she was only under the
impression that she had done so, which is
of course a very different thing. And, in
the second place, as the Fräulein had said,
we are none of us infallible, and it does
not follow because we have thoroughly made
up our minds, that it is not sometimes as
well to reconsider the matter.

As for mere trifles it is best, of course,
to dispose of them for once and for all,
and then to rank them inexorably with
the things which have been. But the very
reason for acting in this way is in itself
a proof that great matters are not to be
decided in a moment. We toss the little

trifles out of the way in order that our mind may be free to concentrate itself upon larger matters. To omnipotence and omniscience, no doubt, the hairs of our head are numbered. But man has other matters to think of than the number of his hairs.

There came one day to Confucius a young mandarin who asked him if he knew the number of the stars. Confucius replied that he troubled himself with things that were nearer to him than the stars. Upon this the young gentleman politely expressed his desire to be informed how many hairs there were in Confucius' pigtail. Hereat the sage lost patience, and answered angrily that he neither knew nor cared.

Next morning almost as soon as the sun

was up, Lord Norwich swung himself out
of his cot and set to work on a letter to
Marcia. A letter is often a most trouble-
some thing. Solicitors, and other—let me
say—men of business, are perfectly aware
of this. If they want to keep you waiting
off and on, to suit their purposes, they
always say, " Write me a letter, and set
out your views and wishes fully."

As a rule, the client is hopelessly unequal to this task. If he is equal to it,
and sends a business-like letter saying
exactly what he wants, and upon what
terms he is willing to have it done, he
gets a reply to the effect that " his favour
is duly to hand, and shall have immediate
consideration."

It has been said that it takes an honest
man to write a good letter; anyhow the

converse of the proposition is usually true.
Here is Lord Norwich's letter to Marcia :

"DEAR MISS CONYERS,

"I deeply regret your determina-
tion, but will not now, at any rate, attempt
to argue it with you.

"I shall not change my own mind, as
time will show you. There are many years
yet to come, and things do not always turn
out either as we wish or as we expect.

"I shall sail to-day for the north—Scot-
land or Norway, as the wind may suit—and
as I want to make sure that this reaches
you, my sailing-master brings it.

"We shall be certain to meet again,
and it is a sincere pleasure added to life
to know that we shall always do so as
true friends. Beyond this always consider

me as a brother, if you should need a brother's services. Fortunately the tide is making, or I might be tempted to write more.

"Kindest regards to Fräulein Dietz.

"Always your most sincere friend,

"NORWICH."

The sailing-master took the letter up, and, pursuant to instructions, waited until he was assured that Miss Conyers had got it, his orders being that it needed no answer. Then he reported himself on board, and steam was up in no time, and the hawsers were cast off, and the 'Cecilia' glided out of the old harbour, with the white ensign of the Squadron at her stern. The last that Marcia saw of her through her glasses was a thin streak of smoke on the blue horizon.

Next day Marcia went as usual to Arques with the Fräulein, but the picture somehow did not get on as well as usual. It was a bad day for colour; and I am a little afraid that Marcia and Miss Dietz had some sort of difference of opinion, which unsympathetic and coarse-minded people might almost have termed a row.

Lord Norwich, for his part, cursed his luck, and made a solemn resolution to dismiss the whole matter from his mind for the present; having done which he thought of nothing else for the remainder of the day, and in fact could hardly keep himself from turning the 'Cecilia's' nose back again to Dieppe.

The Greeks of old called night the kindly one; and he was not sorry when night came.

"After all," he said, "I suppose there
is some one thing or other which every
fellow wants to make him happy, and
which his hard luck has put beyond his
reach. Who the devil am I that I should
be any exception to the rule? It's hard,
though, all the same." Many men, with
an immense reputation for philosophy,
could not have summed up the situation
so concisely.

CHAPTER IX.

A FEW evenings only after the departure of the 'Cecilia,' Marcia and the Fräulein found themselves in the *salon* of the Casino. A capital band was playing its best, and the gleaming parquet was crowded with dancers.

Marcia and her old friend were looking on. It is always pleasant to look on at dancing, even though you may not dance yourself, although you may be fond of dancing, but unable to join the crowd on the floor for want of a partner to your choice, or for some other sufficiently cogent reason.

Suddenly while thus occupied, Marcia became aware that a gentleman was waiting to speak to her, and looking at him she recognized Mr. Quillett, the second partner of the eminent firm which had for many years conducted Sir Hugo's business and enjoyed his confidence, or to use Mr. Quillett's own phrase, listened to his lies for reward in that behalf.

Mr. Quillett, with the happy assurance of a prosperous solicitor, plunged at once into conversation. He was going to England to-morrow. Could he execute any commission for Miss Conyers? He hoped he saw Miss Conyers well. Perhaps he might be permitted to say that she was looking remarkably well. Might he congratulate her most sincerely on her most brilliant success at the Academy? He had seen the picture himself, and although almost entirely ignorant of art, had admired it immensely. It was, if he might say so, lifelike in the extreme, and he had heard from the highest authority that it had secured her a reputation almost unparalleled for so young an aspirant to fame. In fact, Sir Humphrey Courteley, the leader of the Parliamentary Bar, and himself a very distinguished amateur, had said so much in so many words in Mr. Quillett's hearing, and had declared it was a shame that the Royal Academicians should not admit ladies within their magic circle.

"They are jealous, Mr. Quillett," he had said; "they are jealous. Look at Rosa Bonheur; look at Miss Thompson. The women, when they take to painting in earnest, beat the men hollow. So they do on the stage—as honourable and as good a profession as my own. So they do in music. Look at Rachel and Sarah Bernhardt. Look at Dejazet. Look at Madame Norman Neruda. Look at Arabella Goddard." "And I believe he was right, Miss Conyers. In fact I am sure he was," added the old gentleman.

Marcia acknowledged these compliments with that amount of courtesy which she considered their sincerity to deserve, and Mr. Quillett then turned to business.

He particularly wished to introduce her to a gentleman, he might say, or indeed he ought to say, a nobleman, who was an old member of Boodles', and intimately acquainted with her father. It was Lord

Henry Forrester, brother of the Duke of Worcester, and a great enthusiast in all matters of art. Might he do so?

It was difficult to say no. Seated in the *salon* of the Casino, she could hardly plead that she was still in mourning for Sir Hugo, and there was no excuse available that would not have been an obvious falsehood, so she had to say yes.

Lord Henry was a man considerably above the average height, and admirably built. He gave you the idea that in his time he had rowed in the University eight, and that he could still hold his own at any athletic pursuit. He was distinctly handsome, even from a man's point of view. His hair had here and there a few silver streaks, as if to prove that its prevalent jet black was not the product of art.

His heavy moustache was cut short, and his cheeks were closely shaved; for he had features of which any man might have been proud, and was perfectly aware of the fact.

There was no stiffness as of military drill about him, nor on the other hand any slovenliness or peculiar knack of gait, such as that by which we can tell at once the man who can do nothing at all, and feels his limbs a difficulty to him, or on the other hand the man who is always in the saddle or always at sea, and cannot hide the fact. But all Lord Henry's movements told of strength and skill in manly arts. You would probably have conjectured, and not without good reason, that he could take half thirty and a bisque, and hold his own with a professional tennis-player.

Lord Henry was an accomplished talker. On this point Frenchmen deceive themselves. They imagine that they are the best talkers in the world. On the contrary, a well-bred English gentleman has not his equal in conversation, for he is, as a rule, utterly unconscious, or, if conscious, can entirely conceal the fact.

In a very few minutes he had made fully as much progress in Marcia's good opinion as he could have wished, and perhaps even more than he had expected, for he was a novelty to her. He spoke with proper respect, but with no affectation of deep sorrow of his old friend, Sir Hugo, his brilliant abilities, his comparatively retired life, and his sudden death. Then he turned to Art, and without at all flattering Marcia, enabled her at once to see that he understood precisely the strong points in her work, and thoroughly appreciated them.

Then he began to tell her of places which he had seen himself, and which she ought to see—of Sicily, of the Riviera, of the Levant, and of California, where the climate, sky, and sun of the Mediterranean, are united with the grandeur of nature, that is as far beyond anything in the old world, as are the immense peaks of the Andes above the ranges of the Alps and Appenines.

It was impossible not to listen to him, and impossible not to be charmed. He spoke of what he knew. He spoke with what, if not genuine feeling, was at any rate the perfection of art, and he had a peculiar and irresistible grace of manner.

Nor was all this mere acting. Put the character of the man aside, and he was as nearly perfect as a man need be— handsome, as I have said, highly educated, and with a genuine love of nature and of art. Such men, when the opportunity has come to them of using their power, have often left their mark on the history of the world. Cæsar Borgia impressed even Machiavelli. Tiberius, of whom Tacitus writes with a distinctly personal hatred, was a magnificent administrator, and the most accomplished member of his own Court. Charles Edward Stuart has never had justice done him. We might come nearer to our own day. There must be some sort of magic about Don Carlos apart altogether from his heraldic claims, that secures him the staunch allegiance he undoubtedly commands and inspires.

Marcia had of course introduced Lord Henry to the Fräulein, who, forming her own opinion at once, said as little as possible, and in fact succeeded admirably in playing the part of a stupid over-the-middle-age woman, rather tired at being dragged about as chaperone, and extremely indifferent to everything that was going on. In reality the old lady was as wide-awake as a cat when she pretends to go to sleep in the sun on a balustrade commanding the terrace where the pigeons and sparrows are picking up the crumbs that have been thrown for them.

The good lady knew her way about, and although her own life had been entirely innocent of love passages, yet understood men thoroughly—perhaps all the more thoroughly for that very reason.

At last Lord Henry suggested the terrace, the room was getting stifling, he said; and somehow, before she knew it, Marcia found herself on his arm, and out under the moonlight in the delicious evening air. This was the man's opportunity, and he knew how to put it to advantage. To tell the truth, he fascinated Marcia, for the very simple reason that he was more than her match, and in fact more than the match of any man whom she had ever come across. Old Sir Hugo, with all his little arts, not to call them dodges, would have been a mere child in his hands. John Douglas would have had the worst of it in crossing rapiers with him, and would have lost his temper and shown as much, and so with his temper have also lost his game. No good lawyer, that is to say no sound lawyer, is ever a good man of the world. Lord Norwich would have had a better chance, having perfect control over himself, and seeing at once with what manner of man he had to deal. But even he would have found himself outwitted, and have had to choose between conscious defeat or open quarrel.

For myself I do not know how one is to deal with men of this stamp—experienced as Ulysses, clever as Voltaire, and unscrupulous as the first Napoleon. The only thing to do is, if you are where it can be done, and are sure of yourself, to call them out and kill them as unhesitatingly as you would kill a wild beast. And this may seem at the present stage of my story to be what Americans term "a big order." So perhaps the story itself had better go on, and make out my justification.

Out on the terrace Lord Henry talked
apparently of everything under the sun,
and yet somehow made Marcia distinctly
understand that he was as much taken
by her as any man of his age and wisdom
could be. Language, it has been said, is
given you that you may hide your
thoughts. You may carry this idea a step
farther. The most skilful user of language
is the man who, while talking apparently
of nothing in particular, makes you understand of what it is that he is thinking.
And Lord Henry was a man of this
type. He was a master of the art. A
shorthand writer might have taken down
every word he said, and if the transcript had
been read out to a British jury, the twelve
good men and true would have considered
it an ordinary conversation somehow above

their own heads, and have laughed to scorn the idea that it had any undercurrent of meaning. But the undercurrent was there, although the jury would probably not have detected it, even if they had been actually listening. They would only have thought that his lordship was an uncommonly clever and well-informed man who expressed himself uncommonly well and pleasantly.

Marcia, frank, straightforward, and honest as the day, was so charmed that the moments flew, and it was not until the band ceased the final galop that it occurred to her to look at her watch. She had actually been away from the Fräulein more than an hour.

Lord Henry was far too wise to remonstrate against her wish to rejoin the Fräulein. They found that estimable lady

waiting their arrival with a peculiarly
grim expression of countenance, quaintly
at variance with her amiable features, and,
as Marcia could see at once, distinctly out
of temper.

"Shall you be here to-morrow morning?"
asked Lord Henry, in the most natural of
tones as he handed over his charge to
Miss Dietz.

"We go to Arques to-morrow, you
remember, Marcia." So Miss Dietz, inter-
rupting incisively.

But for once in a way Marcia declined
to accept the Fräulein's suggestion.

"Oh yes," she answered, "I think I shall
come down here to-morrow, and freshen
myself again with looking at the sea. One
can easily get into a groove over painting,
and that is neither good for the picture nor

for yourself. My father used to say that regular players never play unless they feel in the vein, and take their holidays almost religiously, about the only trace of self-restraint they possess. Yes, I shall be here to-morrow, Lord Henry."

"I shall look out for you," said Lord Henry.

With this they parted, but when the two ladies were fairly home there ensued what schoolboys profanely term a kick-up. You may call it what you will, for it has many names. "Shindy" perhaps best expresses what occurred, as it conveys the idea of misunderstanding between friends, followed by explanation and reconciliation.

The Fräulein spoke her mind, and stuck to her guns. Marcia was equally frank and equally obstinate. The Fräulein told her young friend she was a child, and that her vanity had been played upon. Marcia retorted the Fräulein had better at once call her a fool, and added something about there having been wise men before Solomon, and brave men before Agamemnon.

The elder lady said that she no more pretended to be Solomon than to be the Queen of Sheba, but that there were some things sufficiently simple to need no Solomon for their elucidation. And she added, that you cannot talk the moon out of the sky, which was appropriate enough, but not exactly original. Marcia replied that if any one were equal to the task of talking the moon out of the sky, with or without a sufficient cause for such an interference with the ordinary course of nature, the

person in question would be Miss Dietz.
And .with this Parthian dart she marched
off to her room.

As she was only angry she was soon
asleep. But the poor Fräulein was
anxious as well as angry, and her sleep
was not what that of the just ought to be,
and the proverb declares it.

CHAPTER X.

FOR some days the breach between Marcia
and the Fräulein showed no sign of mend-
ing. Each lady, the young as well as
the old, had a certain show of reason for
considering herself the aggrieved party,
and holding that she had been very badly
treated.

From the Fräulein's point of view Marcia
was froward and ungrateful. "I have been
like a mother to her," said the little woman
to herself. "No mother could have loved
her daughter better. She knows that all
I do and say is for the very best. And

now, instead of even talking things over
with me, she pushes me on one side as if
I had some motive or object of my own
in the matter. She might at least give
me credit for meaning well. And she
treats me as if I were getting into my
second childhood. It's too bad!" and
the poor little old lady comforted herself
with a good, honest, Teutonic burst of
crying.

Marcia, on the other hand, was in an
extreme state of irritation and wounded
dignity. "Fräulein Dietz," she angrily
thought, "was still no more than a nursery
governess, with very many estimable qualities perhaps; but a nursery governess all
the same. She would like, I believe,"
thought Miss Conyers, "to send me to bed
without my dinner, and to diet me upon

the bread of affliction and the water of affliction. It's perfectly intolerable. First she lectures me about Lord Norwich, and now she is lecturing me again about Lord Henry. Who on earth is Fräulein Dietz that she should be infallible? If she did not really mean well her interference would be downright impertinence, and I don't see for my part that meaning well is always to be taken as an excuse. It's your people who mean well that make all the mischief in the world. And really the Fräulein is becoming quite a nuisance."

And then I am sorry to add that Marcia instituted a series of very irreverent and sarcastic comparisons between the Fräulein and various more or less grotesque objects of nature; such as an old hen cackling after a brood of ducklings which have

joyfully taken to the water; Mrs. Parting-
ton defying the Atlantic with her mop;
and a bumble-bee imprisoned under an
inverted glass and indignant at a confine-
ment the nature of which he is wholly
unable to fathom.

It is thus evident that there was considerable want of forbearance, not to say
of charity, upon each side, or that in the
homely parlance of domestic life, the fat
was in the fire. And the quarrels of
women are worse than those of men. For
when a couple of men have quarrelled and
desire to make matters up, neither of them
insists, or in fact expects, that the other
should humbly own himself to have been
in the wrong; whereas a woman, before she
will forgive you, sticks up the Caudine
Forks, and insists that you shall walk

under them barefooted, your hands bound behind you, and your head submissively bowed.

Now it was not likely that the Fräulein would submit to indignities of this kind to please Marcia, or that Marcia on her side would submit to them to please the Fräulein. So that matters were at a deadlock.

Thus have I often seen in some narrow lane or alley in the city two heavily-laden vans meet in different directions, and the driver of each stand by his guns and refuse to back out for the other. Sometimes from mere opprobrious language the dispute passes over into actual conflict. Sometimes the policeman descends like Zeus and stops the battle.

In the present case unhappily there was

no *deus ex machinâ.* I know what you are
saying to yourself, madam or miss. You
are thinking, only in more courtly phraseology than I can command, that it would
have served the two ladies right to have
taken the one in one hand, and the other
in the other, and to have knocked their
heads together. You are right, ladies, as
you always are. But there was, unfortunately, nobody to thus satisfactorily settle
the matter. Even Thackeray's great Lord
Steyne found it best to leave the ladies
of his household to settle their difficulties
among themselves.

For a week at least things drifted on in
this way. The picture came to a standstill.
The daily visits to Arques were discon-
tinued. Marcia and the Fräulein spoke
to each other as little as possible. The

Fräulein would sit indoors over her knitting, or would take it out with her to the Casino grounds. Marcia would arm herself with a book and also make her way to the Casino, where she would sit at a distance from the Fräulein.

It is needless to say that she and Lord Henry constantly met. That excellent nobleman had not been so smitten during the last dozen years of his valuable and useful life.

Marcia, her sound common sense and usual perspicuity notwithstanding, seemed a perfect child in his hands. The fact is, Lord Henry had completely bewitched her, and for the first time in her life she was really in love. And when a woman of Marcia's temperament really loves a man, it becomes a very serious business indeed.

Lord Henry was absent for three days. He told Marcia that important business with the family lawyer necessitated his presence in Town. Where he had gone and what he was actually doing, may perhaps best be gathered by reproducing a scene that was being enacted at St. Austell Towers, and which will moreover throw a little light on the *ménage* Forrester.

* * * * * *

Drawing-room at St. Austell Towers. Five o'clock tea going on. *Dramatis Personæ*—Lady St. Austell, the Duchess of Lincoln, Lady Lindsay, and Lady Henry Forrester.

The Duchess. When do you expect the happy couple, Lady St. Austell? Ought they not to be here by this time?

Lady St. Austell. I believe they *are* due,

but our local line is so erratic that I never expect people for an hour after their stated time.

Lady Lindsay. Is the bride pretty ?

Lady St. Austell. She had £8000 a year. *C'est tout dire.*

The Duchess. Yes, beauty would have been superfluous. How long have they been married ?

Lady St. Austell. About a month, I think. I know it is their first appearance in public, if one can call one's friends the public.

The Duchess. It was a good match for Lord Cheltenham ; he was up to his eyes in debt.

Lady St. Austell. Well, she got his title, and made her own conditions, and they were pretty hard ones.

The Duchess. Really ? I never heard.

Lady St. Austell. Oh yes; he had to swear he would never gamble again, sell his racehorses, break with a creature in South Belgravia, and give up Mrs. Montagu Foster.

Lady Lindsay. How monstrous of a girl to know of such things! Who can have told her?

Lady St. Austell. The disappointed men, I suppose, who wanted to marry her.

Lady Lindsay. Is it possible a man could be so dishonourable?

Lady Henry Forrester. Ha! ha! men indeed! Lady Lindsay, you surely do not believe in men's honour. It went out long ago, with duelling.

Lady Lindsay. I know some honourable men.

Lady Henry Forrester. Do you? I don't.

Lady Lindsay (*sharply*). Then I wonder you are so fond of their society.

Lady Henry Forrester. They amuse me.

Lady St. Austell (*aside to the Duchess*). And pay her bets.

Duchess. But she always wins. (*Aside to Lady St. Austell.*) How can you have such a woman in the house ?

Lady St. Austell. She amuses St. Austell, and keeps people going. You know she had an *affaire* with Cheltenham ; hence her bitterness.

Duchess. Of course, every one knows that.

Lady St. Austell (*aloud*). I hear a carriage. I suppose they have arrived. Yes ; here they are.

(*Enter* LORD *and* LADY CHELTENHAM.)

Introduction.   Effusive   hand-shaking.

Lady Cheltenham undergoes a volley of ill-bred stares which she bears with the utmost composure.

Lady St. Austell (handing Lady Cheltenham a cup of tea). I suppose it is useless to offer you this non-intoxicating beverage, Lord Cheltenham?

Lord Cheltenham (laughing). On the contrary, I love it. Pray don't imply that I drink.

Lady St. Austell (handing him a cup). No! I only thought you might prefer something else. *(To Lady Cheltenham).* And what sort of journey have you had?

Lady Cheltenham. Detestable—very rainy, and a horridly slow train.

Lord Cheltenham. Fancy a wife, who has only been married a month, calling any journey with her husband detestable!

Lady Cheltenham. It was not your fault, but I have got so sick of travelling. We seem to have lived in railway-carriages for the last month.

Lady St. Austell. You have been to Aix?

Lady Cheltenham. We have been all over the continent, and I never wish to see the interior of a church again.

Lord Cheltenham. What an impious remark!

Lady Lindsay (to the Duchess, sotto voce). I daresay she wishes she had never seen one with him! She appears to have a temper.

Duchess. So has he; he won't stand much of that sort of thing.

Lady Henry Forrester (in a soft tone to Lord Cheltenham, who has sat down on a small ottoman beside her). My congratulations come very late, but you must nevertheless accept them. I was at Luchon when I heard of your marriage.

Lord Cheltenham (smiling). You are very kind.

Lady Henry Forrester (to Lord Cheltenham). She is very handsome. (*Lord Cheltenham shrugs his shoulders.*) But she is, as you will soon find out when other men make love to her.

Lord Cheltenham. I don't think they *will.* Lady Cheltenham has principles, and has not been spoilt by the world : she is only twenty.

Lady Henry Forrester. Really ? I must still further congratulate you then.

Lord Cheltenham. It is perfectly true ; she very much dislikes flirting married women.

Lady Henry Forrester. And had

£200,000 ! Where did you *dénicher* a treasure combining so many excellent qualities ?

Lord Cheltenham. I met her at Woolston.

Lady Henry Forrester (*hesitatingly*). And has she made you share her opinion about flirting married women ?

Lord Cheltenham. I never cared but for one married woman.

Lady Henry Forrester. One at a time, I suppose you mean.

Lord Cheltenham. You know perfectly well what I mean.

Lady Henry Forrester (*laughing and rising*). The conversation is getting personal. I will go and change my dress.

The Duchess (*to Lady Lindsay*). How indecent of that woman to carry him off before he has been in the room five minutes !

Lady Lindsay. My dear Duchess, French-women are all alike; they cannot exist without admiration and excitement. She will make that poor young thing perfectly miserable.

The Duchess. Lord Cheltenham will scarcely be fool enough to prefer her painted face to the bright English beauty of his wife — for she really is good-looking.

Lady Cheltenham (to Lady St. Austell). Have you many people in the house, Lady St. Austell?

Lady St. Austell. You have seen all our party with the exception of the men.

Lady Cheltenham. Who is that French lady? I did not catch her name.

Lady St. Austell. She is Lady Henry Forrester—an amusing little woman.

Q 2

Lady Lindsay. I never heard her say anything amusing.

The Duchess. She keeps it for her admirers, who, I am bound to say, appear fully to appreciate it.

Lady Cheltenham. But her husband?

Lady St. Austell. Oh, I fancy that Lord Henry and ·she understand one another. Anyhow, he never seems to turn up. She is of excellent family. She was a Beauregard, you know.

Lady Lindsay. She is very unpopular.

Lord Cheltenham. With women.

Lady St. Austell. I like her. I think she is harmless; silly, perhaps; but my husband is devoted to her.

Lady Lindsay. I believe most people's husbands are; she has a *culte* for them.

Lady St. Austell. Lady Lindsay, you are

positively uncharitable. The dressing-bell
has gone some time; we must really go
and adorn ourselves.

(*Enter servant with card which he hands to*
Lady St. Austell.)

Lady St. Austell (*reading card*). Lord
Henry Forrester! Well, this is talking of
the devil and seeing his hoofs with a
vengeance!

Lady Lindsay. You don't mean to say
that Lord Henry has turned up? (*Aside to
the Duchess.*) A fortunate thing for Lady
Cheltenham.

Lady St. Austell (*to servant*). Show this
gentleman into the study, and let Lady
Henry be told that some one wishes to see
her.

FRAGMENTS OF CONVERSATION BETWEEN THE FORRESTERS.

Lord Henry. Ah, tu ne veux pas m'envoyer une misère de 50,000 francs. Eh bien, nous allons voir !

Lady Henry. Je n'ai que dix mille francs au monde, mais prends les, et de grâce va t'en. Je t'enverrai d'avantage demain.

Lord Henry. Tu le jures ?

Lady Henry. Lord Cheltenham est ici—cela te suffit-il ?

IN THE DRAWING-ROOM BEFORE DINNER.

Lady Lindsay (to Lady Henry). And so at last we are to have the pleasure of seeing Lord Henry ?

Lady Henry Forrester. I am afraid not. He only came on most important business.

Lady St. Austell. But he has not gone, surely!

Lady Henry Forrester. Alas! He begged me to make every excuse possible, but he was obliged to catch the night train to London. You know diplomats are not their own masters. He starts for St. Petersburg to-morrow.

Lord Cheltenham (aside). A little journey that will cost me a thousand or two, I'll be bound.

* * * * * *

Lord Cheltenham seated writing letters in morning-room at St. Austell Towers.

Lady Cheltenham (entering). Lord St. Austell was asking for you. Have you not finished your letters yet?

Lord Cheltenham (impatiently, and hastily covering over a note he is writing). I am nearly ready. I was going out with St. Austell, but if he is in a hurry, he can start without me.

Lady Cheltenham. Your correspondence seems very important this morning (*catching sight of cheque-book on table*). Who have you been writing cheques for?

Lord Cheltenham. My dear Amy, curiosity is not only the sin that lost the whole world, but it is an extremely vulgar vice. What can it interest you to know which of my tradesmen I have been paying?

Lady Cheltenham. It does not interest me in the slightest. Shall I put your letters in the bag?

Lord Cheltenham. Yes, you can take these (*gives her a packet, and carefully places one in his breast-pocket*).

Lady Cheltenham. Is not that one to go?

Lord Cheltenham. No, it's of no consequence—it's not quite finished—and now
I must be off. Are you going to remain
here?

Lady Cheltenham. Yes, I have some letters
to write. I suppose I must let people know
where I am.

Lord Cheltenham. Good-bye then.

(*Exit* LORD CHELTENHAM.)

Lady Cheltenham (soliloquising). I must
break off this entanglement he has with
that horrid little Frenchwoman at once.
And yet how is it to be done? I cannot
make a scene, but I will not put up with
her insolence and airs of condescension to
me. She was perfectly odious last night
with her airs of proprietorship and mock
humility. I wonder if that note that he

has so carefully hidden from me is intended
for her. It would be very wrong to hold
up the blotting-paper to the looking-glass,
I suppose; what my husband would call
a vulgar vice (*holds blotting-paper hesitatingly
in her hand*). It is early days to begin
suspicion and jealousy, but if he is carrying
on an intrigue with that woman I am
determined she shall be exposed (*holds the
paper up to the looking-glass and reads
fragments*). "Dear Berthe—sorry for your
trouble—enclose—you ask for—no repeti-
tion—" Berthe! that must be that vile
woman, and yet what can she have asked
him for? Surely not money? (*Turns the
paper about and reads* "£1000.") A thousand pounds! How disgraceful! How in-
famous!—he gives a woman a thousand
pounds who is staying in the very house

with his wife (*suppresses tears*). No, I will not cry. I will tell her I know all, and insist on her leaving the house at once. (*Rings the bell. To servant.*) Please let Lady Henry Forrester know that I wish particularly to see her here for a few minutes.

Enter LADY HENRY FORRESTER.

Lady Henry Forrester. Ah! dear Lady Cheltenham—how cold these country-houses are with their long, dreary passages—did you wish to speak to me?

Lady Cheltenham. I will be plain with you, Lady Henry. I have discovered, I need not tell you how, that you have renewed the—intrigue you had with my husband before my marriage.

Lady Henry Forrester (*insolently*). Après.

Lady Cheltenham. He gave you a cheque for £1000 this morning, and I sent for you to tell you that you either leave this house to-day, or I expose your conduct to Lady St. Austell.

Lady Henry Forrester. Mon Dieu! what a storm in a tea-cup! Intrigue! Exposure! Expulsion! Disgrace! What delicious heroics! My dear Lady Cheltenham, you were not intended for the present generation. You ought to have lived in the days of Arcadian shepherdesses, you are so delightfully simple. My intrigue, as you call it, with your husband, consists of some valuable state secrets which my husband procured, Heaven knows how—for I don't understand these things—and which he brought down, just having paid for them the sum in question on behalf of your husband, who was most anxious to obtain the information.

Lady Cheltenham. A most plausible explanation, I must admit, Lady Henry. But unfortunately I happen to have read the note which accompanied the cheque ; and though I will not discuss with you the services you have rendered my husband, as you have been fully paid for them, I am sure you will see the wisdom of leaving this house.

Lady Henry Forrester (*wincing*). You are very cruel, Lady Cheltenham. I could explain everything — (*recovering herself*). However, having paid a high price for your husband you are perhaps right to be *exigéante.*

Lady Cheltenham. I am not *exigéante,* but I am disappointed, as I thought I had paid *all* his debts when I married him.

(*Enter* LADY ST. AUSTELL *and the* DUCHESS *of* LINCOLN.)

Lady St. Austell. My dear Lady Cheltenham, I have been looking for you everywhere. What have you two been talking about? The inevitable toilette, I suppose.

Lady Cheltenham (*looking Lady Henry full in the face*). Lady Henry has been making me her adieux, and I believe was just going to seek for you. She has had bad news. Her husband, you know, is going abroad, and she does not like to leave him alone.

The Duchess (*aside*). She certainly never leaves other people's husbands alone. What can have happened?

Lady St. Austell. I am most distressed. Is it imperative that you should go?

Lady Henry Forrester. I am afraid it is

(*smiling*). You know—La femme doit suivre son mari.

The Duchess (*aside*). Yes, but you generally follow some one else's, which I expect is your present little game.

Lady Henry Forrester. You must make all my excuses to *ces messieurs*. I am afraid they will not return before I leave. (*To Lady Cheltenham.*) My best compliments to your husband. I dare say his *diplomatic* business will soon call him to town, and then I may have the pleasure of seeing him. Dear Lady St. Austell, you must soon come up to my little *bicoque* in Park Street and do a week's plays. Duchess, it is only *au revoir;* I shall meet you in Paris in October. (*Sotto voce to Lady Cheltenham.*) Quant à toi, vipère : je te repincerai plus tard.

(*Exit* LADY HENRY.)

Lady St. Austell and the Duchess (together to Lady Cheltenham). You have gained a glorious victory. What does it all mean?

Lady Cheltenham. It means simply that Lady Henry has got the *nostalgie du foyer*, and is returning to her disconsolate husband.

The Duchess. But they are never together by any chance.

Lady Cheltenham. Well, I would rather not discuss her—she really interests me so very little.

BEFORE DINNER IN LORD AND LADY CHELTENHAM'S DRESSING-ROOM.

Lord Cheltenham (angrily). And you dared to turn her out of the house! You showed a lamentable want of taste. However, the degradation was for you, who placed your-self in a most humiliating position.

Lady Cheltenham. I was *placed*, you mean.

Lord Cheltenham. You have no self-respect. How did you get hold of my note ?

Lady Cheltenham (laughing). That will only be revealed with other important secrets on the judgment-day !

Lord Cheltenham. You must learn once for all that I will not be interfered with.

Lady Cheltenham. Then you must carry on your *liaisons* with greater caution in future. I decline to be outraged by the presence of a woman like Lady Henry Forrester in any house in which I am staying (*descends to drawing-room smiling*).

* * * * * *

The Fräulein hated the whole affair. She had thoroughly distrusted Lord Henry from the first, and was all the more incensed against him for being the cause of her difference with Marcia, and the gulf that seemed daily widening between them.

The landlady of the house at which they lodged noticed the estrangement, and spoke of it with much gesticulation and even tears in her eyes to her husband François. François, being in his way a philosopher, replied that no woman ever knew her own mind.

> "Souvent femme varie
> Bien folle qui s'y fie."

Madame told her husband that he was a pig of a brute. The good man chuckled, lit his cigarette, and went down to his favourite *cabaret*, where he sat down to console himself with a glass of vin ordinaire and water.

Now it so happened that there sat down

by him an Englishman, evidently to the experienced eye a gentleman's gentleman, who produced a meerschaum pipe, cursed French tobacco, and mixed himself some cognac and seltzer.

He was very pleasant, was this same Englishman, and not at all reserved or awkward, like most of his compatriots. In fact, before long he and François were on the best of terms, and François had told him all the little news of Dieppe, including that of his own household, in which he felt sure his new acquaintance would take an absorbing interest, the whole thing being so very droll.

The stranger was a capital listener. François, who was hardly allowed to open his mouth at home, rather prided himself upon his conversational faculties; and very probably the two might have gone on talking until now, had not the Englishman suddenly discovered that he had stopped too long already in such good company, and that he would be in all probability soundly rated by his governor. So he paid the reckoning as a hospitable man should, and strolled away, gently whistling to himself a once popular air, the words of which refer to the hopeless passion of a broken-hearted milkman, resident in the neighbourhood of Paddington Green, which he somehow seemed to find consonant with his own meditations.

When he reached the Hôtel Royal he walked straight through the small court-yard, and making his way to Lord Henry, who was standing under the verandah, respectfully touched his hat. There was no one as it happened within earshot.

" Well, Peters ? "

" I've seen the husband, my lord, and he's told me as much as he knows, and I think that's about all. Miss Conyers and the old lady have been quarrelling, and are now hardly on speaking terms. The landlady's sorry for this, as she doesn't of course want to lose steady regular paying lodgers who give no trouble. The husband doesn't know what the quarrel is about, and says he doesn't care. The two ladies, as a rule, always used to go out together, but now they generally go out separate. The old lady looked to-day as if she'd been crying, and Miss Conyers, so the husband said, looked ferocious. That was his word, my lord."

" Very well, Peters, you can go."

So Peters went, or rather vanished unobtrusively, as a servant who knows his work ought, and Lord Henry strolled down to the Casino. There, under the awning on the terrace facing the sea was Marcia, with a volume of Tennyson, which she was not reading. Fräulein Dietz was nowhere visible.

"I am so glad you have come," said Marcia. "It is dreadfully dull here alone."

"Then why stay? I am sick of the place myself. The races are over, everybody is going, and I should have gone long ago myself if it had not been for you. Let us go straight to Paris this very afternoon. You have promised to marry me, why delay it? We can be married in the Embassy at once. I suppose we are both of age."

Marcia laughed. Then she began to trace

imaginary figures on the ground with the point of her parasol.

"There is a train at four," continued Lord Henry. "It is now only two. Never mind about packing, or anything of that sort. We shall be in Paris shortly after eight, and you can get anything you want there in a moment."

Marcia hesitated for some few seconds. Then she looked up in her own fearless manner, shook her head as if to shake down the tresses of her hair, and after one more second said, "Yes, we will go."

She rose from her chair and they walked side by side out of the Casino grounds into the Grand Rue. Here some slight purchases were made, and they soon found themselves at the station.

There was no trouble or worry about

tickets or any other such preparations.
Mr. Peters with an immovable face had
got everything ready. A *coupé* had been
secured. In it there was fruit and wine
and a large caraffe of frozen water, and
an entire assortment of journals. Before
Marcia had fairly looked round her and
taken her seat, the train had started.

From Dieppe to Paris is but a trifle over
four hours. The day was one of those
glorious summer days which are only to
be had along the coast of France. The
country was at its best and fairest. To
Marcia, now thoroughly happy, it seemed
full of new beauties. She did not feel
inclined to talk, and her companion guessed
her mood, hardly speaking, except now
and then to call attention to some old
village church or quaint farm-house, some

river vista of the Seine flowing peacefully seawards.

The shadows lengthened; the clouds began to fall. The swallows were flying low. Soon came the suburbs, and then the fortifications, and then as the train drew up at the St. Lazare Station, the door was opened by the ever-attentive Mr. Peters, and Lord Henry swinging himself down to the platform held out his hands and assisted Marcia to descend.

A good valet is a jewel far beyond the average of rubies. There was a brougham waiting, and in a moment Lord Henry and Marcia were being driven rapidly along the busy Boulevards to the Grand Hotel. Their arrival had been expected, and rooms were ready for them.

There was a chambermaid of superior

grade, who quietly and quickly took upon herself the functions of lady's-maid, arranged Marcia's hair, and as far as was possible assisted her, so skilfully and effectively, that Marcia herself, as she looked at her own reflection in the tall cheval glass, could hardly believe that she had but just arrived from a hurried journey.

A single blossom of white stephanotis in her hair, and a spray of the same flower at the side of her circular Scotch brooch, completed the toilet.

Women do not dress to please other women. They dress to annoy other women —to exasperate them if you will—and to please men. Marcia, as I have said long ago, had an almost faultless taste in dress, and on this occasion she was fully satisfied with her own appearance.

Lastly, the maid handed her a box of gloves, from which Marcia selected the pair that best harmonized with her dress. So she passed through a corridor which the maid pointed out, and found herself in a large *salon* brilliantly lighted and exquisitely decorated with flowers.

In one corner of the room was a grand piano, and by it a low case filled with music. Here and there in niches or on pedestals were statues of Parian. Her feet sank into the carpet. The fireplace was filled with strange and beautiful ferns. The open windows looked out on to a balcony fitted with cushions, carpeted and furnished, the whole covered in with a great Venetian tent of red and white, through the drawn curtain of which could be seen the broad Boulevards des Capucines full of motion and life.

Marcia turned to Lord Henry, held out both her hands to him, and said, "It is beautiful. Thank you, Henry, for all your thoughtfulness."

"You light a dull old place up, my sweetheart," he answered, "like a diamond in the depths of a mine." And he put his arms round her, gently pressed her head down on his broad chest, and gave her a long deep kiss between her eyes.

END OF VOL. II.